Saving
LUCIE
COLE

OTHER BOOKS BY LYNNE LARSON

In the Shadow of an Angel

LYNNE LARSON

Saving
LUCIE
A NOVEL COLE

Covenant Communications, Inc.

Cover foreground figure: *A New Beginning* © Mike Malm. For more information visit www.mikemalm. com. Cover background scenic: *Golden Sky* by Jon McNaughton © McNaughton Fine Art Co. For more information visit www.jonmcnaughton.com.

Cover design copyright © 2014 by Covenant Communications, Inc.

Published by Covenant Communications, Inc.
American Fork, Utah

Printed in the United States of America
First Printing: January 2014

19 18 17 16 15 14   10 9 8 7 6 5 4 3 2 1

ISBN 978-1-62108-499-0

For Brittany A. Chapman, a proud direct descendent of Ruth May Fox and her daughter Lucy Beryl.

Introduction

THERE'S A STORY THAT'S COME down through the decades about a young woman who endured a horrible crisis in the wilderness of Southern Utah. It happened back in the days when folks traveled by wagon through the dust and thistles of lonely country trails and washed-out gullies. Their carriage wheels sank into sifting red sand, the sun beat in their faces, and danger of all kinds seemed to lurk at every turn—wild animals, desert dust storms, suspicious-looking strangers, or simply a mirage of anxiety that could be just as lethal. Maybe that's all this story was from the very beginning—a mirage. But it's a tale to tell, and every good tale has a purpose.

According to the legend, Ruth May Fox, an extraordinary church-woman and longtime general Young Ladies MIA counselor and president, figured in the events, which is appropriate because Sister Fox knew all about the dangers and anxieties of mortality. She traveled the waste and wilderness of Utah for nearly forty years, striving to protect her beloved "young ladies" from anything that would hurt them or lead them from the righteous path.

But, as I say, it's an undocumented legend, this story you're about to read; it may not be true at all. Some chroniclers tend toward the dramatic in their remembrances. A daring rescue? A threatening stranger? Shadows in the desert twilight? A mysterious old woman coming to the aid of the faithful victims? Perhaps it was all just a dream simmering up like scorching heat in the annals of Western lore and anecdote. But if the legend doesn't precisely follow the facts, so be it. Stories don't have to *be* true to *teach* what's true, and the poet in Ruth

May Fox would certainly vouch for that. Ruth knew her allegories and metaphors, and she knew a great deal more. "If it didn't happen that way, it should have," she often said, only half in jest.

Yes, she was quite a woman, this "Grand Lady of the MIA." The *Church News* gave Ruth that title in 1953 when the paper noted her 100th birthday. She walked across the plains as a girl, married at nineteen, and bore twelve children in Zion. She labored with national feminist organizations on behalf of women's suffrage, and she worked tirelessly to ensure that Utah's state constitution included women's right to vote. She went on to serve for thirty-nine years as a general officer with the YWMIA and was general president from 1929 to 1937. She lived to be 104 and was still going strong by the time airplanes replaced wagons and trains for distant Church assignments. Neither deserts nor oceans could stop her when it came to representing the Church in the far corners of the world. She addressed cottage meetings, dedications, and firesides. She was one of the first women to speak in the Salt Lake Tabernacle at a general conference session. Ruth was a friend of the famous, including Eliza R. Snow and Emmeline B. Wells, but she was not above washing and sewing and cooking for any local Relief Society president she met in the backwater camps and rural villages of Utah. That was Ruth May Fox. Oddly enough, we might have forgotten the great lady by now if she hadn't also written a song, "Firm as the Mountains around Us," or "Carry On," as some like to call it. Either title—as well as this tale—appropriately eulogize Ruth and remind us through myth and metaphor just how remarkable she was.

Chapter One
ON THE ROAD

Beware the stalker, be he real or imagined. He lives in the shadows, watching and following, intensely aware of our vulnerable moments in this mortal wilderness.

EARLY ON A DRY JUNE morning in 1903, three travelers appeared at the wagon yard just off Tabernacle Street in St. George, Utah. Two of them stood together in the shade of the depot porch, waiting patiently for Tom Leavitt, the freight driver, to load their bags into the high, six-seat carriage that would take them the sixty-five miles north to Modena, Utah, and the rail line there. Modena was the nearest train connection for passengers from St. George bound for Salt Lake City and points north, and Leavitt ran a brisk business, meeting the Southern Pacific at least three days a week with goods and travelers. He was a large, solid man with heavy features and sweat seeping through his shirt, but he treated his customers like friends and made constant efforts toward their comfort. "We'll have you on board in no time." He tipped his crumpled hat to the lady and the gentleman who stood by as he hustled his preparations, knowing special people were in his care today.

The woman was middle aged and striking in appearance, with piercing brown eyes and the posture of a queen. She wore the stylish shirtwaist of the period and a trim little jacket in spite of the Dixie heat. Her pocketed skirt was straight and ankle length, and her shoes, which sneaked out at the bottom, were leather, low heeled, and buttoned. She'd borrowed a stiff straw hat for the journey—although pinned cloches of velvet usually suited her—for she was determined to keep her soft, rosy cheeks out of the sun. She smiled easily and watched Leavitt with great interest as he checked and rechecked the harness straps and buckles on the four-horse team. Two tall boys in billed caps moved freight to the carriage—trunks, boxes, even a barrel of salt, in addition to the luggage of the prospective passengers. A freight customer was fussing with the cart boys about one particular trunk, and Leavitt came to settle things. "Now, Sister Cottam," he said with patient indulgence to the matronly owner of the luggage, "you know I'll take good care of your quilts. That trunk will make it just fine to Modena." The two onlookers smiled at the commotion over the trunk. Apparently, Leavitt had dealt with Sister Cottam before. She backed away, still sputtering nervously about her quilts but willing to let the teamster have the last word.

"He seems as good with people's feelings as he is with his freight," the woman in the straw hat whispered to her companion, impressed with Leavitt's handling of the situation.

The man who accompanied the woman in the straw hat was much younger than she, slight in build, solicitous, and well dressed. He wore wire-rim spectacles and had the habit of often removing them, wiping the lenses with his handkerchief, and carefully replacing the stems over his ears, only to remove them again at the first whiff of dust. It was plain to see that the Dixie sun did not suit him, but he remained patient as his collar tightened and chafed and as beads of sweat dripped down his back.

"I'm sure you may take your coat off, Brother Meade, once we've started," offered the woman, sympathizing with him. "Somehow the desert defies decorum, and I shall not be offended in the least."

Meade nodded nervously, thinking of his suspenders fastened with a large safety pin on one side. Somehow on their long journey, he'd lost the proper snap. "Thank you, Sister Fox," he said, "but I am fine."

Their attention soon turned to a young woman standing nearby who would undoubtedly travel with them. She was tearfully saying good-bye to a full-bosomed older companion and a host of friends who had arrived at the gate. Everyone within earshot was taken with the moment.

Sister Fox nudged the man in the spectacles. "Look how pretty she is, Fenton," she said, nodding toward the girl. "She reminds me of my own daughters at home, all dewy and bright-eyed." Dressed for travel, the girl wore a linen skirt, fashionably belted, topped by a blouse and tunic, which fit her slim figure precisely and revealed a high-starched collar pinned with a bow. Her hair was chestnut colored. It had been piled high in a fashionable twist and fastened with pearl combs. She wore no hat, and her high cheeks showed a blush of sunburn. Her large eyes, wet with tears, were full of light. This, apparently, was no ordinary day.

"Oh, Aunt Caroline," the girl wailed, "and all of you . . . how shall I ever get through the next month without you?" There were hugs and whispers and then more laughter to accompany the tears. "You will come to the wedding? You promised!"

Several of her friends nodded eagerly in reply, and the older woman answered out loud for all of them. "You're our angel," she said gaily, "and your wedding day will be as precious to me as my own. I would never miss being there."

"A month from now, we'll be descending on Salt Lake City en masse," echoed one of the others in the circle. "Everyone in town will know that the girls from Dixie have arrived. And you better save us room in your bridal line, or we'll have to invade it! We're country tough, you know, and used to claiming our place."

This brought more laughter before a serious tone began to dominate. "Honest, Lucie," wept one of the young women, "we'll miss you an awfully lot."

"But we're mighty happy for you," another hurried to add. "Your Albert is a dandy. We can't wait to see him all gussied up."

Aunt Caroline came front and center then, and Lucie's friends stepped back reluctantly. "You've been like my own daughter," the woman said, placing her hands on the girl's shoulders. "I feel like I'm sending you away too soon, even if it is for the best of reasons."

They embraced again, and Lucie whimpered, "Oh, Auntie, I'll miss you so," and she reached to touch the woman's cheek and then to squeeze the hands of all who were there to bid farewell.

"I promised these girls' mothers I'd have them back in time to help with the ward picnic," Aunt Caroline finally said regretfully. "But we'll see you soon, remember." She turned quickly to keep from giving way to further tears, and amidst a chorus of good-byes, she and the girls moved slowly to the gate, waving back once more before they disappeared. The young woman stood looking after them for several seconds, and when she turned to gather herself and her belongings, she met the sympathetic smiles of Brother Meade and Sister Fox, who had been interested observers of the scene.

"Parting is indeed sweet sorrow," murmured Sister Fox to Fenton Meade, and he nodded amiably.

The girl dropped her eyes, and her cheeks flushed a little upon seeing that her emotional farewells had been overheard. She recognized the woman standing there. She finally stepped forward and sheepishly put out her hand. "You're Sister Ruth May Fox, aren't you? And I'm so ashamed to be in tears when it looks as though I'll be sharing a carriage ride with you. I can hardly believe it."

"Perhaps a train ride too," said Sister Fox brightly. "From what I overheard, we're both going to Salt Lake." She took the girl's hand in hers and pressed it firmly. "And you're to be married soon. What a privilege it is for me to accompany a bride." She put her arm across the girl's shoulder and guided her into the shade of the porch as the young man followed. "This is Brother Fenton Meade," Sister Fox turned to introduce him, "my companion on this journey, and now, it appears he's yours as well."

The girl and Brother Meade shook hands. "I'm Lucie Cole," she said as the fellow tipped his hat. Turning back to Sister Fox, she added, "I heard you speak yesterday in the Tabernacle. You were wonderful."

"It's the gospel that's wonderful, my dear, but you're a jewel to flatter an old lady."

Lucie *had* heard Ruth Fox speak, and Ruth looked at her now and imagined her sitting in the balcony of the St. George Tabernacle the day before, listening politely. Ruth hoped she had given this young woman something that had nourished her soul. A thousand mothers and daughters sat before her at that special conference. She brought greetings from the Young Ladies general board in Salt Lake City, and she'd tried to make the sisters of Dixie feel that they were never forgotten here in their southern outpost. Ruth humbly knew that she was a celebrity among the leaders of the YLMIA and always drew a crowd wherever she traveled. But had she really touched this Lucie with her message, or had the girl listened more out of respect than eagerness?

Lucie Cole was still chatting with enthusiasm when Tom Leavitt called for them to board. "I can't believe my own good fortune!" she bubbled. "Wait till I tell everyone I got to travel home with Ruth May Fox."

Ruth smiled and held tightly to Lucie's arm. The girl may have felt a coveted connection, but the woman, too, was pleased. *What a delight she is*, Ruth thought, and she looked forward to the journey with this young bride-to-be. "I hope you'll let me call you Lucie," she said brightly. "With so many miles to go together, I doubt that we'll be strangers very long."

***

Across the road from the wagon yard, hidden in the shadows of a clutter of sheds, another stranger stood watching Leavitt's passengers as they prepared to leave. He was husky and broad shouldered with a short dark beard and a ragged, weather-beaten look that labeled him a vagrant. But his dull gray eyes followed every motion of the travelers who climbed aboard the carriage. Once they were seated and their attention taken up with getting settled for the journey, the man stepped into the open to spit tobacco juice from the side of his mouth, though his attention remained fixed on the wagon yard. An old wrangler lugging a halter passed by, and the bearded stranger stopped him, asking offhandedly, "That transit carriage there, where's it headed? Do ya know?"

The wrangler paused to squint querulously at the wagon yard, known for its daily dust and traffic. "That's Tom Leavitt's carriage," he said. "Bound for Modena, I expect. Meets the Salt Lake train there two, three days a week." Not bothering to look at the stranger, he lifted the halter to his shoulder. "Yeah, Tom'll take ya to Modena.

But it'll cost ya. Runs a tight business, Tom does." He moved away, indifferent about the man who'd questioned him, and the stranger let him go with no reply. His gray eyes had never left the wagon yard, and now a soft smile played along his lips as he again ducked out of sight.

*****

The carriage was a hard-covered surrey, mercifully protecting its passengers from the direct rays of the sun. It was larger than either Ruth or Lucie had expected. Fenton Meade had courteously helped the ladies into their seats and then taken his own place facing them. When the coach lurched away from the depot, four eager horses trotted forth, their harness jangling and the lines snapping. The passengers were grateful for the padded seats and the backrests the carriage afforded. The two passenger sections had been built atop a spring wagon, braced on the sides and raised so that the center of the wagon box could be used for freight. The women and Brother Meade were in the first compartment. Luggage and freight filled the space behind them, where two more seats were available had there been more passengers. But most of the baggage was packed underneath the carriage in the wagon box, including a trunk of Sister Cottam's quilts, five of them, headed to a Mormon Handicraft shop in Salt Lake City. All told, the load was heavy, even with minimal riders. Flinty Tom Leavitt sat midway above them on the driver's seat, a plank with little padding and only a small back rail. He urged the horses on with growls and whistles and took the bounce of the buckboard like the veteran driver that he was.

In a fleeting moment, they turned onto the main street and were heading past all of the familiar St. George landmarks—the black ridge; the red sandstone boulders on the bluff; the wide avenues below, where adobe houses stood on gardened, tree-lined lots, sun-drenched, watered, and well-groomed. The mild winter and the mellow air left the fields and orchards abundant by this time of year, the long growing season making up for the harsh, burning wilderness that lay outside the city. The Virgin and Santa Clara Rivers were the lifeblood of Dixie, and the people had made the most of their treasure.

Both Ruth and Lucie turned to find the temple one last time. They could see pieces of it through the trees and houses to the south, stunningly white and regal. Easier to take in was the Tabernacle, which they soon passed directly on the left and where Ruth had addressed the women the day before.

Ruth had affection for the pioneer building with its red brick; tall, multi-paned windows; and white New England clock and steeple. How the people of St. George loved their tabernacle, a symbol of all their parents and grandparents had accomplished. She felt Lucie's hand tighten on her wrist as they passed by and found her companion looking appreciatively at the building too.

"You did give a beautiful talk yesterday, Sister Fox," said the girl. "Was it your first time in the tabernacle?"

"Oh no. I've been here many times." Ruth's thoughts remained on the receding view of the building as she spoke. "But it's always special. It never gets old."

"The same could be said for you, Sister Fox," said Fenton Meade in the seat across from them, and the woman chuckled, accepting the compliment graciously.

Under more rising bluffs, the carriage rattled along the Santa Clara and through the farmland and orchards below the red mountain, so striking and ominous in its barren beauty. Beyond it was Snow Canyon, studded with cliffs of pink and gold and orange flame. "My friends and I liked to hike and picnic there." Lucie pointed toward the canyon. "We'd explore the high boulders and ledges just as Paiutes did a thousand years ago. The view is breathtaking."

Ruth nodded. She had long delighted in the Western landscape and was pleased to see that Lucie felt the same. The fertile setting of St. George turned to wilderness very quickly. Old Jacob Hamlin's tall adobe house was the last one on the road leading from Santa Clara, and rock and sagebrush rose up soon after that. The Pine Valley Mountains loomed ahead of them, shuttering the northeastern sky. Livestock foraged in the few meadows that remained, and birds and wildlife dominated the land. A human being felt small against this landscape.

"Tell us, Sister Ruth," said Meade as he looked about, "does the isolation of this country bother you? I mean, it's so desolate out here."

"I've seen it all before," Ruth answered, smiling. "It's desolate all right, but there's a beauty to it just the same."

"I don't suppose it will ever be worth much, monetarily speaking," returned the young man. "There's not enough water here to wet a whistle." This brought appreciative smiles from the women, and Fenton Meade leaned back in his seat, pleased with himself.

Ruth looked with interest at Lucie Cole. The girl was engrossed in the panorama, though she still clung tightly to Ruth's arm. *Sweet girl! She's only starting out, a young woman with her entire life ahead of her, and here am I, just like those Paiutes she spoke of. I feel like I've been around a thousand years.* Ruth was tired and underestimating her own beauty. The crow's feet were evident and the cleft in her chin more sharply etched. But her skin was soft and lovely, almost luminescent, and the eyes—oh, the eyes! They were full of sparkle, people told her. "Seeing eyes," her grandmother would have called them. They seemed to reflect a deep fascination of whatever came into view. There was nothing lazy nor languid about them, nothing at all. Ruth thought of her words to her audience the day before. *"You of the noble birthright,"* she had admonished, *"be true to virtues for which your parents sacrificed. Be strong in the faith. Hold fast to that which is good. Have courage and the Lord will devour the serpent for thy sake. The evil of the world will never harm you. 'Be thou humble; and the Lord thy God shall lead thee by the hand, and give thee answers to thy prayers.'"*

She hoped Lucie remembered those words particularly, and she glanced again—with a touch of curiosity—at the girl. Suddenly, the image of the Lord devouring the serpent seemed oddly appropriate since they were now crossing a wasteland probably filled with serpents. She wondered if Lucie would appreciate the metaphor. Neither one of them was a physical match for any real horrors that the natural world might present. Still, this young woman seemed to feel secure beside her. Ruth hoped that she exuded spiritual strength and courage in spite of her other limitations.

But this was a young bride-to-be, and it was time to talk of other things.

"So," Ruth began cheerily, when the road had straightened, "you must tell us about your young man."

"Oh, I'd love to." Lucie smiled. "His name is Albert Covington. His friends call him Al or Bert or Bertie, but I like Albert. It's distinguished, don't you think? He's an elder in the Church and a returned missionary. Here, I have his picture if you'd like to see." She fumbled in her little purse and brought out a flat silver case the size of a playing card. On the inside of its lid was a small photograph of a jaunty young man with thick blond hair and a broad smile. The bottom of the case was lined by a calendar, and with it, a little pencil held in place by a delicate chain. The pencil was red at one end and black at the other, and it was plain to see which color she preferred.

"They're all red-letter days," said Meade pleasantly, noticing the dates Lucie had marked.

"Oh, yes," answered Lucie. "I've been crossing them off since I've been down here, and red is the perfect color."

"Perhaps you should simply jump ahead, marking all the days until the wedding," suggested Meade. "Who knows? It might make the time go faster."

"Oh no, I couldn't do that," laughed Lucie. "My mother says it's bad luck to scratch off days you haven't come to yet. It's like cutting your life short before you've lived it. Isn't that right, Sister Fox?"

"It certainly is," affirmed Ruth, looking approvingly at Albert Covington's beaming face in the photograph. She carefully handed the case back. "He's a handsome young man, Lucie, and you're right. With a good husband, they're all red-letter days."

"We're to be married the first day of July," continued Lucie. "My mother has a reception planned. She says she'll string lights on all our fence posts and on the gate and arbor; there will be flowers every-where and long tables spread with roasted beef and turkey, salads, crepes, and custard. She says bands will play music throughout the house. My father says he'll have to *sell* the house to pay for it!"

Ruth and Fenton Meade laughed at Lucie's enthusiasm, appreci-ating it.

The carriage bounced and swayed over the worst of a washed-out section of the road, which was layered with sand up to the spokes.

Dust whirled through the open sides and onto the women's dresses, making them gritty and soiled. The heat caused their collars and sleeves to moisten, turning the dust to grime. Brother Meade loosened his tie and unbuttoned his collar, pleading the ladies' pardon, and finally moved up onto the seat beside Tom Leavitt, thinking the women might feel more free to remove their jackets if they were alone in the compartment. "Take a seat, bud," they heard Leavitt say cheerfully to Meade. "I never mind the company if you don't mind the bounce."

"Is Brother Meade your bodyguard?" Lucie whispered to Ruth when the man was out of earshot. Her tone was intimate and naïve and brought a smile from the older woman, who was fanning herself with a palm-leaf fan.

"*Escort* is a better word," she answered. "The Church insists that we sisters are always accompanied in our travels by at least one gentleman for our protection." There was a note of sarcasm on the word *protection*, and Ruth's wink reaffirmed it.

"He looks more like a clerk than a policeman," Lucie giggled. "How safe are we, Sister Fox?"

Ruth's eyes danced with spritely humor. "He *is* a clerk, dear girl! There were no General Authorities available, so they sent poor Fenton, who would rather be anywhere but here."

"Is he a married man?"

"Oh, yes, and with a new baby he's anxious to get home to. Brother Fenton is small in stature, but he has reason to prod the driver along."

Ruth wiped her face with her handkerchief, and Lucie helped her remove her jacket before taking off her own. The sun was hidden by the canvas carriage cover, but heat seeped in like dust, soon leaving curls and collars limp and Ruth's palm-fan waving at a generous pace. Lucie felt sorry for her. "Have you been long on the road, Sister Fox? Was our meeting in St. George your last stop?"

"I left Salt Lake a little over three weeks ago but only went as far as Marysvale on the train. Since then we've covered some 300 miles by team and wagon—Junction, Panguitch, Hatchtown, Kanab, Orderville—we've been all over."

"Three weeks?" Lucie was amazed.

"Oh, I love the little towns. The leaders there, they are always so grateful to have anyone from Salt Lake, and the girls—oh, the girls—we must take care of them, you know. They are lost in small, isolated places without much chance for good education and worthy companions. We worry about them, and that's why I make these journeys." Her mind drifted a little as she mused. "I made it into Arizona this time," she said. "A little place called Moccasin about twenty miles from Kanab. It's a lovely little spot. We spent the night and then moved on to Pipe Springs, where Brigham Young established a telegraph station back in the day. The first town back in Utah was Grafton, a poor dead little settlement with only three girls. Oh, how I wanted to take them in my arms, poor little things. The gospel seems far away in Grafton."

The carriage lurched from side to side as Leavitt urged the horses through another graveled washout. "Sorry, ladies!" he called down from the high buckboard, and Meade nervously gripped whatever he could lay his hands on. Lucie held her breath until the wheels found level ruts again.

"The people need warming up spiritually." Sister Fox went on fanning. "We stayed with Bishop Cutler in Glendale. I helped with the sewing. Actually, it had been so long since Brother Meade had had a change of underwear, I sat right down and used some homespun Sister Cutler had to make him a pair of long johns—but don't tell him I mentioned it. We ironed too and washed. Of course, we always help with the cooking. It's the least we can do when we descend on these people—help with the cooking. We often eat outside, you know, and Brother Meade hauls water and sets up tables and such. Yes, I help with all the meals, and if there're girls on hand, I try to teach them a thing or two about big city etiquette that maybe their mothers forgot."

Lucie smiled at that. Her own mother was a tyrant about good manners, and now she felt a new affection for the cause.

"President Wooley in Kanab actually got us tickets to a play they were having there," Ruth Fox continued. "*Better than Gold*, it was called, and a nice little presentation. Of course, I've had a wonderful time these last few days in St. George. I went to the Relief Society conference before I spoke to you young women. President Rulon

Wells was there with his sister Annie Wells Cannon. They are headed on down to Arizona now. Seems like we're all at cross paths if not cross purposes."

Ruth paused, realizing she was monopolizing the conversation.

"But here I am, running on about myself," she finally said. "You're the one with exciting news. You've got your Albert and a wedding very soon." She studied Lucie for a moment. "You've been lonely without him, haven't you?"

Lucie hesitated, but Ruth's friendliness was genuine and invited intimacy. "I've been in St. George attending school and living with my Aunt Caroline while Albert finished at the BY Academy." She paused again and then added with a blush, "Our parents deemed it wise for us to spend some time apart, both to test our feelings and to protect our virtue, once our desires became serious." Ruth smiled, and Lucie added quickly, "I can truthfully say that both have remained intact."

"Three cheers for Dixie!" said Ruth with a wry wink, and Lucie appreciated the woman for responding to a serious subject with twinkling wit. "What is your Albert going into?" was Ruth's next question. "An interesting career, I hope."

"Business and manufacturing," replied Lucie proudly. "He sees a future in parts for automobiles now that they're beginning to appear more in Salt Lake. He thinks they're the coming thing."

"Oh, they are," said Ruth. "Brother Meade has one, you know. A strange-looking little carriage with an engine that spits smoke. But he loves it. I think he's forgotten how to ride a horse, if he ever knew."

"Perhaps you'll use one in your travels for the Church someday," mused Lucie. "Albert says we'll all have them before long, and that can't hurt his career."

"And what about you?" asked Ruth. "Any work that interests you before the babies come?"

Lucie blushed at the remark. "I love to sing and do theatricals," she said. "Albert wants me to continue to perform whenever I can and teach our children to do the same. He sees the beauty in it."

"How marvelous," Ruth answered, delighted. "I wish I had your talent. I may write songs someday, but I've no voice to perform them, certainly not in a theater. No, my youth was much less elegant. I worked in a woolen mill when I was eighteen. I ran a machine just like a man, and I wanted to be paid like a man. My father, who ran the mill, thought I was worth it, but he didn't want to upset his partner, so we settled on ten dollars a week—still good money for a girl. But I never forgot the inequality. I used to speak a lot at various places in the early nineties when we were pushing for statehood. We wanted to make certain that our new constitution included suffrage, so I worked hard for that. I was the treasurer of the Utah Territorial Women Suffrage Association back then, you know, and there was no let up in what we had to do. I was a ward Primary counselor at the same time, nineteen years altogether. But the children—the children needed nurturing and teaching. And now it's the young women. Young women like you, Lucie. Oh, I've loved them all. I remember one time I was on my way to Logan . . ."

Ruth chattered on, and Lucie listened, and the hours passed away under the Dixie sun.

The carriage had traveled ten miles when Tom Leavitt pulled the horses up to a small grove of junipers just off the trail. A thin stream gurgled nearby, providing a bit of grass and water for the team. Leavitt brought cups and canteens for the passengers and spread a wool blanket on the ground so they could sit. After tending to the horses, he provided sandwiches for lunch and regaled Meade and the women with stories of the area. Never had any of them seen a land more desolate. Craggy boulders and ledges surrounded them. An ocean of sagebrush and prickly desert flora spread out on either side with only an occasional cedar or Joshua tree to mark the horizon. The sun was like brass, gleaming relentlessly with nothing to soften its shine.

"The Southern Pacific sidetracked St. George when it turned off west into Nevada," Leavitt told them. "But from Modena, the rails go all the way to California and Los Angeles. It's quite a thing. I'm sure Sister Fox can remember when the railroad ended at St. Louis. Folks bound for Utah or California had to ride an oxcart."

"Or walk, as I did!" exclaimed Ruth proudly.

Leavitt nodded respectfully. "It's an honor to have you along today, Sister Fox," he said sincerely. "You folks who came out here before the railroad should never be forgotten. If I can do anything to make you more comfortable, just let me know. It's not an easy path through this prairie in the heat."

"Mr. Leavitt," said Ruth, chin up, "if I can make it from St. Louis to the Valley, I can make it from St. George to Modena! Don't you fret about me."

After finishing the sandwiches, the group lingered in the shade, reluctant to climb aboard the carriage again. The others pressed Sister Fox to tell her story. She fell into a contemplative mood, and they listened quietly, mesmerized by her voice.

"I was born in England and never knew my mother since she'd died in childbirth when I was eighteen months old." Ruth rested against a cushion from the carriage as she talked, and there amidst the sandstone cliffs, images of the past took hold. "My father came to America first, and then he sent for us, my sister and me. I was five years old. We settled in Philadelphia with relatives for a time. But Father had joined the Church in the old country, and we longed to go to Zion. I was thirteen when we finally made the trek, going first by train to St. Louis and then by team and wagon across the prairie to the Rocky Mountains. I must be honest. When I first saw the Salt Lake Valley, I was disappointed. This was the promised Zion? It was so harsh and rugged and dusty. I had been used to Philadelphia, you know, where we had paved streets and fine theaters and shops. But it didn't take long for me to fall in love with the mountains, the streams, the canyons. Zion is the home of the Saints and truly the valley our Father loves."

Ruth's three listeners were silent, not wishing to break her spell. So she continued, directing her words mostly toward Lucie. "I married Jesse Fox in 1873, when I was nineteen. Yes, thirty years ago! Now, I've given away my age," Ruth laughed softly. "We've had twelve children and our share of challenges, but I'm happy in my marriage and in the service of the Lord. Zion's youth are my greatest concern, next to my own family. I taught in the Primary for a good long time, and I've worked on the board in the general YLMIA under Sister Elmina Taylor for five years now. I expect to keep at it for as long as I'm needed. I can put up with anything for the girls and the gospel . . .

even the Dixie sun!" She laughed again, a melodic, gentle laugh, which was self-effacing in spite of all she'd obviously accomplished.

Alone in the minimal shade of the cedar trees, listening to the ripple of the stream and feeling the vastness of the isolated prairie, Tom Leavitt, the husky carriage driver, looked long and hard at Sister Fox. Affected by her story, he cleared his throat and declared, "I don't think you should be out here, ma'am. You're near fifty years old, and you've already crossed a prairie. Look at you. You must weigh all of a hundred pounds. I got all the respect in the world for the Church and the Brethren, but you've done your part and done it well. I mean no offense, Sister Fox, but surely it's someone else's turn to forge out here in the wild, lookin' after the girls in all these woebegone little towns. That's my view, anyway, and I've said it."

"I've promised to fulfill my calling, Brother Leavitt," replied Ruth. There was not much conviction in her voice, for she was tired and there was a part of her that appreciated the teamster's concern and agreed with his assessment.

When they finally gathered themselves to return to the carriage, Leavitt made extra efforts to help the women and ensure their comfort. He felt he had spoken out of turn. He helped Ruth into her seat with care, speaking sheepishly as he did so. "I hope you'll pardon my words, ma'am. I'm a crusty fellow and used to hard labor. It's what these thick arms 'r for. Men like me, we're responsible for the likes of you and the little gal there. It don't seem right sometimes for a genteel lady to take on the desert. That's all."

Ruth nodded with a smile and squeezed the driver's hand before she took her seat. She did indeed feel safe and secure in his charge, far more than she did with Fenton Meade, whose job it was to protect her. She'd never complain—she liked Meade. He was a loyal, strict, methodical young man who knew his duty. But his collar was tight, and his glasses always needed cleaning. She had the feeling that Tom Leavitt would lay down his life for his friends, while Fenton Meade would simply lie down and hope for the best.

And so these four travelers made their way on the dusty Modena road in 1903, each one with secrets and feelings, each with opinions and doubts, and each oblivious to the fate that lay before them. Each oblivious to the gray-eyed stranger who had watched their departure from St. George.

Chapter Two
THE SHADOW RIDER

ANOTHER FIVE MILES PASSED BEFORE Tom Leavitt noticed that they weren't alone. The team had struggled out of a rocky gap where clusters of juniper and sage lined the wheel ruts. They had reached the higher ground where the trail curved blindly around a mass of boulders, and Tom glanced back to check the progress of the carriage. That was when he saw behind them a lone man on a horse, steadily gaining ground from perhaps a mile away. "Looks like we've got company," he said without concern to Fenton Meade, who was still beside him on the buckboard.

The women in the carriage heard Leavitt's words, which were shouted above the noise of the horses, and soon Ruth was pointing out the rider—a dark figure in the distance. Lucie squinted and shaded her eyes, curious about a traveler who was apparently willing to bear the hot sun without a carriage cover.

"Who do you suppose it is?" asked Meade. "Some rancher headed for Modena?"

"I dunno," Leavitt answered casually. "I know most of the ol' boys tryin' to scratch a livin' out here. Could be any of 'em. Ain't close enough to tell. Up here a ways, we'll pull over and see if he wants to tie on and join us, or just go around."

The approach of the rider, moving steadily closer at a measured gait, captured the interest of the carriage passengers. The road was rough and monotonous. The man, whoever he was, was a curiosity, and the eyes of the travelers followed him out of simple inquisitiveness.

They surmised that he was one of them, a merchant perhaps—what some folks called a drummer—bound as they were for the northbound Salt Lake train. For several minutes they watched as he eased his animal through the sage and juniper patches and over the scattered chip rock and sand of the narrow trail they had recently passed. When he got about two hundred yards from the back of the carriage, Ruth could see that he wore a gray or tan slack-brimmed hat and a black coat, which looked heavy on him in the heat. She was anxious for him to come more sharply into view, for she thought she saw a red scarf or bandana around his neck, and the flash of color on so lonesome a creature aroused her interest. The odd thing was the man never got closer to the carriage than the imaginary two hundred–yard barrier. Though Leavitt purposely slowed the carriage two or three times, for the rider to either join them or go around, the man only pulled up on his bridle and paused, keeping his self-determined distance. When Leavitt whipped the horses again, the man followed but never closed the ranks.

"Hoaa! You back there!" called Leavitt at one point. "Tie up your mount and come aboard. Give me a hand with the freight in Modena, and I won't charge you for the ride."

The man held steady on his horse, which circled about in the sage grass, but came no closer. Its rider waited in silence, his eyes on the carriage, as Leavitt tried again: "The road widens a little bit once we get into this next stretch. You can go around us then with no worry. I'll slide to the right at a good spot." But the rider neither waved nor shouted an acknowledgement. He merely waited. And when Leavitt sat down again and the horses jumped forward and found their customary rhythm, the stranger followed at his usual pace, two hundred yards away, his face just out of sight.

Fenton Meade climbed back down into the carriage and began looking nervously underneath the seats opposite the women. As he searched, he kept one eye on the distant rider, popping up every few seconds to check the stranger's progress. Sister Fox grew agitated. "Brother Meade, what on earth are you looking for?"

"Leavitt says there's a rifle here under the seat. A Henry .44." Meade paused to deliberately remove his glasses, wipe the lenses, and then carefully place the stems again over his ears. He looked anxiously back at the rider before finally bending to pull the gun out from under the bench. "Here," he said as Lucie gasped. "The thing is," poor Meade added, "I've never fired one of these things before."

"I have," said Ruth with determination. She took the Henry from Fenton's nervous hands and laid it gingerly against the empty seat. It was a big rifle, heavier than she remembered, but comfortingly familiar. Still, she refused to believe it was necessary. "Surely, you're overreacting, Brother Meade. A lone rider who doesn't seem to want to come near us? Maybe he doesn't like company. Maybe he's unsure of the route and would rather have us take the lead. He's made no threat. I'd say you and Mr. Leavitt are worried over nothing."

Fenton Meade stared anxiously at the women and then looked back at the rider, still steadily following. Meade was sweating and jittery, and with a quick embarrassed glance at Lucie, he darted out of the compartment and back up to the buckboard with the driver, leaving the rifle behind in the seat.

"Where's the gun?" they heard Leavitt ask and then, "Oh, never mind. Just so we know it's handy."

Lucie looked from the distant figure to Ruth and back again. She stared at the rifle resting nearby. She was wide-eyed and curious. "Who do you suppose he is, Sister Fox?" she finally whispered.

"I don't know," said Ruth, "but I'm not having Fenton handle a gun in these cramped quarters. Heavenly days! We'd have more to fear from that than some innocuous rider on the trail!"

"That man *is* acting strangely, refusing to come close the way he does. You're not worried . . . ?"

Ruth looked at her well-dressed companion and spoke to her frankly. "Yes, I'm worried . . . a little. Perhaps *uneasy* is a better word. There's an old saying—'a stranger in the wilderness may be friend or foe, but until you meet him face-to-face, you'll probably never know.'" Ruth smiled reassuringly. "We're jumping to conclusions here, Lucie. This is 1903. Indians and bandits have faded into the storybooks. Besides, Tom Leavitt knows what he's doing. He'll get us to Modena."

The women kept a curious eye on the mysterious traveler behind them, but both tried to stay calm. The man, whoever he was, might have been odd, but he was not necessarily dangerous. Ruth's practical courage held sway for the moment over the anxiety of Brother Meade.

Another three miles passed with the stranger still keeping his distance while remaining very much in sight. So routine did this pattern become that the passengers and driver began to ignore him. Even Fenton took time to survey the landscape in front of the horses rather than continually twisting his neck for a backward view. The flat prairie had turned once again to rocks and swales and crooked routes which sideswiped dominant bluffs. Clumps of trees occasionally showed where water was or had been. But the vast, primitive scene continued to spread before the little carriage like a dry ocean of red and white waste, bristling with grit and sand and shimmering with heat.

Ruth dozed a little, and when she woke she found Lucie sleeping too, her head against Ruth's shoulder. She looked quickly to the rear and saw, to her mild surprise, that the rider who had been haunting them was gone. The road behind the carriage was empty as far as she could see, with only the dust rising from the wheels. Ruth felt some relief. The rider had not threatened them, but he had been a nuisance with his odd, standoffish demeanor. She reached up and knocked on the back of the driver's seat, and when Fenton and Tom Leavitt turned, she raised her thumb, smiling at them through the rails.

"All clear, Sister Fox," called Leavitt brightly.

Ruth patted the girl's cheek gently so as not to wake her. Ruth indeed felt a connection with this young woman, this soon-to-be bride. Ruth had a "Lucy" of her own at home, still a "kid" at thirteen but old enough to be good help with the household while her mother was away. Lucy Beryl Fox. They called her Beryl, but her name was Lucy too, just like this pretty young thing sleeping now through the bumpy ride.

Ruth loved her girls. She loved the young women of the Church. But as she watched this Lucie, Ruth thought of her daughters and wondered again if she really had accomplished anything in these journeys that took her away from her family for weeks at a time. Most of the country girls she met would go on with their small-town lives whether or not Ruth May Fox had visited their youth conferences.

Train, team, wagon, carriage. Miles and miles of dust and wind, heat and cold. She remembered coming upon a schoolhouse in Marysvale one Sunday where they spent the meeting time trying to get a fire started in an old potbelly stove with a faulty flue. There was no speech that morning, only a great huddling together as the young women tried to keep warm. Maybe that's what it was. A great need for touch and warmth and human connection whether the themes of the great conferences lingered long at all. Maybe that's why her travels were important. Maybe that's why her speeches were essential long after the words were all but forgotten.

Lost in her musings, Ruth didn't realize immediately that the carriage was slowing down, that the horses were sputtering, wheezing, and pulling at their bits, until the wheels finally stopped. Lucie jerked upright as Ruth moved to look around the side of the window frame. She shot a glance behind her and saw nothing, and then she heard a harsh command from the other direction. The man who had followed behind for so many miles was now twenty yards up the trail, directly in front of them. He was larger than he had appeared at a distance, beefy and broad shouldered with thick arms and thighs. A red scarf was tied around his throat, and his beard made his face dark and menacing under his hat. A rifle they hadn't seen before lay across his saddle. The weapon was pointed nowhere in particular, but it gave the stranger leverage, and he spoke peremptorily and with no hesitation.

"I want the girl," he shouted. "Leave her, and the rest of ya can move on to Modena." A heavy silence met the man's words as if all the vast landscape had caught its breath and stopped to listen.

Dumbstruck, Tom Leavitt rose slowly from the buckboard, the harness lines still in his hands. Fenton didn't move. His fingers gripped the side rail near his seat. "What did you say?" Leavitt stared out at the man and could barely find his voice.

"You heard me," growled the rider. "I want the girl. The rest of ya can be on yer way."

Leavitt gathered his wits and answered sharply, "I don't know what you been drinkin', mister, but you ain't gettin' no girl. Now give us the road, lessin' you want a whole lotta trouble on your hands."

In the carriage, Ruth involuntarily gripped Lucie's wrist as she kept her eyes on the figure in their path. Lucie made no sound, but Ruth felt her tremble slightly and then turn rigid as they waited. With her free hand, Ruth felt around for the rifle in the other seat. She was aware of her own heart pounding in her temples, in her chest, in her wrists. She held Lucie all the tighter.

The stranger settled back in his saddle, fingering his weapon. He looked hard at the team and carriage and then eased his horse toward them, moving to the side and closer to the carriage window. His eyes fell on Lucie as she sat stiffly looking on, and Ruth immediately placed herself between the girl and the man's line of vision, keeping Lucie behind her. The man merely grinned at the gesture, an evil, lascivious grin that infuriated Leavitt. "You'd better git on your way, mister. I got a Colt's revolver here that's quicker than your tree limb of a rifle. I'll use it too, you go sniffing around my passengers!"

The stranger curled his lip at Leavitt's threat and seemed to chuckle to himself. His red bandana fluttered in the air. The color looked out of place, for the man was grimy and shabbily clothed—his overall appearance wretched. Ruth fingered the Henry rifle, waiting . . . waiting. The next move was the stranger's, and she expected him to pounce. The way he looked at Lucie made Ruth ill, and under her breath she vowed to use the Henry if he touched the carriage door.

But after a moment the man seemed to change his mind. He smiled, as if his threats were all a tasteless joke, though not one of the travelers was laughing. Every eye followed the stranger as he circled the carriage. Then he turned his horse and guided it through the brush on the other side of the team, giving it a wide berth as he rode past, soon a diminishing figure among the rising cliffs.

The four of them warily watched him go. Tom asked for the Henry, which Ruth still clutched beside her on the seat. She shoved it up to him, stock first through the rail of the buckboard. There was no Colt's revolver, she surmised but said nothing, still catching her breath. She squinted hard at the path the stranger had taken. In only seconds he'd disappeared into the shimmering mirage of the desert with its sandstone ledges and bluffs and its endless vista of waste. But she knew he wasn't far away.

Nervously the men climbed down and helped the ladies from the carriage. Leavitt remained alert, constantly scanning the horizon for any sign of the rider. Meade got water for the women, and Ruth led Lucie to the nearest overhang where some slight shade could be found. The girl sipped slowly from her cup and stared nervously in the direction they had come. "Did you know that man?" asked Ruth.

"I've never seen him before in my life," said Lucie stoutly. Her lips were quivering, but her shoulders remained straight. "Perhaps he's mistaken about who he thinks I am. I don't know what he could possibly want with me."

There was grit in the girl's voice, which Ruth appreciated, but naïveté too. Ruth left her under the cliff and joined the men by the wagon. "Do you think he'll come back?" she asked Leavitt. "Was he familiar to you?"

"Naw, I don't know him, the son of a—pardon, ma'am." Leavitt took off his hat and brushed the sweat from his brow. He paced a little, cursing under his breath. Meade was quiet, shrugging his shoulders when Ruth questioned him about what he may have seen. He was nervous but empty of ideas, and when he finally moved off to splash water on his face and wipe his spectacles, Tom took Ruth aside. "I don't know who that fella was, and I don't know if he'll come back. We're about thirty miles from Modena, maybe a little more. I'd like to cut a horse from the team and send your Brother Meade on ahead for help, but that puts us two short: one man, one horse. I've got a feeling you'd be worth two of Brother Meade, but I don't like giving up the horse."

"I don't know if Meade can manage a horse without a saddle anyway," said Ruth frankly. "He actually drives an automobile at home, one of those crank Fords that spits oil and gasoline fumes all over."

"Well, I guess that answers that." Leavitt was perturbed. An automobile! He had two women and a dandy who couldn't ride a horse. What was next? "I don't mean to worry you, Sister Fox, but this is the only road to Modena. There's no other way."

"And there's no Colt's revolver." Ruth's brows tightened.

Leavitt shook his head and growled again. "Naw, I got no Colt. All we got's the Henry . . . one rifle, and we don't know what he's got besides that barrel across his saddle." Leavitt nodded toward Lucie, still sitting, head bowed, under the cliff ledge. "Does she know this fella? Is he some relation she's runnin' from?"

"No. This girl is bound for Salt Lake to get married. She's not from Dixie. She has no idea who he is."

"Well, I don't neither, but I'll tell you this much, Sister Fox, there's no way he's threatenin' my passengers. I've been driving this route for nearly ten years. I brought Lorenzo Snow from Modena down to St. George the year he promised the Saints rain, and I took him back again too. I had special cargo then, and I got special cargo now, so don't you and that little girl worry. We'll make our thirty miles and the Salt Lake train, whether that fella keeps doggin' us or not!"

With this declaration, Tom was anxious to leave. He quickly checked the harness lines and the wheels. Then he shifted the freight, tossing out a heavy trunk and a barrel of flour. "I can pick this stuff up on the way back," he said, eyeing what was left in the luggage compartment. Sister Cottam's quilts remained, as did a small barrel of salt, a bundle of hides, and some farm implements bound for a hardware store in Salt Lake. Most of the rest belonged to Lucie, who was bringing a great deal home after the entire winter in St. George— two large trunks and a hatbox, together with a case of wedding silver. These things Leavitt reluctantly left on board. Speed was his object, and the less weight, the better. But he disliked being governed by fear, and Miss Lucie's luggage was important to her. He wasn't going to leave it behind.

Ruth brought Lucie back to the carriage, and Fenton helped her in. He turned to Ruth with the same intent, when Leavitt stopped him. "Let's keep both ladies with a masculine companion," he suggested. "You ride inside with the girl, Brother Meade, if Sister Fox don't mind comin' up top with me."

Sister Fox didn't mind at all. Holding her straw hat with one hand, she let Leavitt pull her up to the high seat above the wagon box. It had been too long since she had driven a team of horses. A varnished buggy, maybe, with a single bay wearing blinders. But a four-horse team from a high buckboard seat? Aw, yes! She was young again and relished the thought. Tom Leavitt, she knew, was making the switch to rid himself of the useless Fenton Meade, but Ruth appreciated the gesture. Lucie looked initially alarmed but quickly smiled politely at poor Brother Meade as he climbed into the carriage. "Crack the whip, Mr. Leavitt!" Ruth cried eagerly, remembering another long-ago summer on the open range.

"Yes, ma'am!" roared Tom, and the carriage lurched forward, its iron wheels grinding over the ruts of a thousand wagons before them, although with more urgency than the others. Thirty miles. Ruth had traveled three hundred on this journey alone.

The lone rider was but an aberration. He was nowhere to be seen now. Perhaps he had been a bored wrangler playing a trick. Perhaps he was merely measuring them up, hoping to find an easy mark. Leavitt's thunder had turned him away, making him think better of whatever he had in mind. Ruth hung on to the buckboard rail and thought of a hundred different reasons for what had occurred, measuring each by the urgency in Leavitt's whip.

The land on either side of the road was a lake of dust, studded with sharp cliffs of red and copper and gold on the horizon. On such a trail the four travelers pressed on toward Modena. They were all nervous. Leavitt drove the team with one eye cocked for trouble. He kept the horses at a steady gallop. Even as the miles passed with no sign of the stranger, he made no effort to slow their pace until they reached a muddy trough of water running in a sparse stream bed rimmed by a few cedar trees and some fennel weed. There, the panting animals drank and rested, although Tom hand-watered them, leaving the team in full harness. Ruth checked on Lucie and found her engaged in polite company with Fenton, making conversation, trying to pretend that the unsettling incident with the stranger had never happened. Lucie's free and easy manner had tightened nonetheless. Being threatened on a lonely road with only fellow travelers to count on for help was a daunting business. Ruth looked at the girl with sympathy even as the danger seemed to have passed. "This has taken a toll on our little Lucie," Ruth remarked to Tom once they'd started up again, "but she's being chin-up about it." Ruth tried to imagine the girl happy and well nurtured in a tree-lined Salt Lake City neighborhood, the temple down the street, the lovely canyons at her back, and a loving family offering security and refuge from every danger, spiritual and otherwise. *Maybe she picked up some grit along the way*, Ruth thought and hoped Lucie's stoicism would last.

On the road again, Tom seemed to relax a bit. He put the whip aside and reined the horses at a moderate pace. "I think we lost that fella, whoever he was," he told Ruth, jostling beside him. "I don't know whether it was my whip or your prayers that done it for us, Sister Fox, but I expect it didn't hurt to have 'em both."

Ruth liked Tom Leavitt. He was salty tongued and barrel-chested, and his crumpled hat was greasy from long use. His features were thick, and scraggly whiskers fringed his jowls. His belly hung over his belt, and he desperately needed the thick suspenders that kept his khaki pants at his waist. He was a rough-looking man with few refinements, and he kept a book of matches in his shirt pocket, probably for a pipe or cigar when he wasn't in the company of ladies or Lorenzo Snow. Ruth didn't care to know. This man was competent in his work and good with his horses, and Ruth sensed in him a dignity and respect toward women and toward sacred things he didn't totally understand. She felt safe and protected in his charge.

"Are you a native of Dixie, Brother Leavitt?" she asked when the driver took a drink from his canteen. "This seems to be your country."

"My folks were among the first band of settlers in the early sixties. I was a toddler when they come, so I don't remember much about it, but I've tramped these deserts ever since—Gunlock, Escalante, up north to Cedar. I've been all over. It's a brutal country, ma'am, too dry, too harsh, too much grit for civilized people, but there's a beauty here as well." He pointed to a mesa in the distance, which was almost violet against the white midday sky. "Look out there," he said. "The colors can change in a blink and turn all smudged and shadowy, or a storm can come roaring down that valley over yonder and wash the haze away until everything's as clear as glass." Leavitt turned, a little embarrassed by his poetic tone. "It gets ahold of you, this land, with all its space and vastness. But it's darn hard to scrape out a life."

"The Church loves Dixie, Brother Leavitt," said Ruth softly. "You have a temple here, the first in Utah. The Lord sent His best people to build it. You have a heritage to be proud of."

"I've never married, Sister Fox." Tom's voice became serious. "I never was much to look at as far as the ladies were concerned. I'm kinda like the country, I guess—too harsh for gentle skin and touch. And I got no use for civilized courtesies that make a fella sorta weak, to my way of thinkin'. But when that man came and made a threat toward that little girl, I swelled up inside. I couldn't stand it. I don't go to church much anymore, but when someone takes a punch at our people, I feel the same way as I did with that stranger. I swell up inside. Women and the gospel, Sister Fox. Both are sacred to me, whether I always act like it or not."

Ruth answered gently and felt comfortable using the man's first name. She had a newfound fondness for the roughshod Dixie teamster. "Lucie will make it to her wedding, Tom, and she'll have you to thank for it. And I'll live to preach again to Zion's girls, and I'll never forget the day you got me safely to Modena. We all have a place, you know."

The road ahead looked straight and sure, and Tom responded to Ruth's words with a smile and a vigorous slap of the lines on the horses. The team leaped forward in unison, and the carriage squeaked and rattled under its load. Like a ribbon, the distant path wound and twisted behind a spate of jagged rocks. Ruth finally sat back against the rail of the buckboard and enjoyed the ride. The light breeze cooled her cheeks and piqued the odor of desert sage. With one hand she held her straw hat in place, and with the other she gripped the rail. The cloudless sky spread out before them like an illustration anchored by the sandstone hills.

Conquer your fears on this earthly journey. Yes, that was her message to countless audiences throughout the state and beyond—conquer the deserts of mortality with faith, diligence, and devotion. But the girls she cared for, Ruth knew, were only faces in a huge congregation, no different from those in the next town or county, and destined to fade from her memory like so many congregations before. Now here was Lucie Cole, a stranger, a happenstance traveling companion, and yet one of her own. The YLMIA with a face. Ruth thought of Lucie as the carriage rumbled along. Lucie was one of thousands, yet one who was specifically threatened—not with spiritual digression but with something far more physically dangerous. This type of adversity was new to Ruth. Crime and its ugliness had never touched her. She had conquered the wilderness. She had conquered ignorance. But she had never encountered an enemy like this.

Suddenly the road began to curve and pitch, and clumps of trees and boulders sprang on one side and then the other. Leavitt slowed a bit to maneuver the team around a stand of cedars hugging the road. The trail's edge skirted the top of a dry wash, the site of flash flooding during a sudden storm but now as scorched as sandpaper. The wash furrowed a gully along the road for quarter of a mile, cutting a vertical swath about twenty feet below them on one side. Almost without warning the heavy carriage began to lose its grip on the wagon tracks beneath it. Something ahead had made the horses shudder and the iron wheels whip sideways, and Tom Leavitt was suddenly fighting gravity with all his power to keep the outfit upright on the road. Ruth's face turned white. She gripped the rail with both hands, and her heart froze in terror. She couldn't breathe, and in the next instant, the sky began to turn. The horses struggled to avoid catastrophe, even as Tom struggled with the lines.

In its panic, the team stumbled out of stride. The front horses lost their footing in the sand and caused the pair behind them to skid and whine. The carriage veered dangerously to the right again. Tom shouted and growled and worked to keep the wheels on level ground. But the wash was steep and the edge too soft, and the last thing Ruth remembered was the grip of Tom's fist on the strap and the tight set of his jaw as he tried to save them.

It was a futile effort. The carriage seemed to hang for one brief pulsebeat in the air, poised to fly. But with no wings—nor any road to hold its wheels—it fell sideways, bounced against the gully's gravel edge, and lurched downward, landing overturned at the bottom of the furrow in a tremendous clatter of wreckage and rising dust. Amid the screams and groans, Ruth lost all sense of direction and reality until she saw her straw hat sailing down the gully like a kite. Pain shot through her. In five short seconds, life had turned to rubble on the Modena road.

***

Dazed and battered, Ruth opened her eyes to a white sky and saw a flaming sun staring back, blinding her. She was lying in a gravelly patch of greasewood, hot and brittle to the touch. When she tried to move, her shoulder throbbed, sending shock waves to her fingers. Her joints seemed knotted and twisted, and when she was finally able to lift herself, she managed only to roll onto her side before lightheadedness forced her to her back again. She squinted into the sun, confused and nauseated by the pain. Ten seconds ago she was sitting on a wagon seat, trying to keep a straw hat from blowing off. Now, there was no hat and no wagon to be seen. Trunks and suitcases were scattered about the wash. Dust hung like powder in the air. Then Ruth became aware of the sound of a horse snorting and sputtering nearby. Someone or something was clamoring through the debris, and soon a shadow blotted out the sun.

"Sister Fox! Oh, no, no, no! Sister Fox!"

It was Fenton. She knew his voice, and suddenly he was hovering around her like a frightened sparrow, darting this way and that in her blurred line of vision. "Oh, Sister Fox!" he repeated, and Ruth struggled to one elbow, feeling sorry for the man. She was all right and couldn't stand his fussing. He tried to put something under her head, a cushion or a folded coat, but she gripped his arm and pulled herself forward. Her senses were still spinning. She was scratched and bruised, yet she knew she was alive and had urgent work to do. Strange how long habits and deeply burnished traits come to the fore in times of stress and injury. At first disoriented, in another moment Ruth was frantically pleading with Meade to let her up. Someone needed her.

"Lucie! Where is Lucie?" she gasped. Meade made an effort to settle her, but she sat straight up, still gripping him. "Is Lucie all right?"

"Lucy's fine, Sister Fox. She's waiting in Salt Lake."

Poor boy, thought Ruth, *he thinks I'm dotty. He thinks I've lost my mind, crying for my daughter, my own dear Lucy at home. But it's another Lucie who needs me now.* "Miss Cole, Brother Meade, the young woman with us. Is she all right?"

"I haven't found her," said Fenton sheepishly, "nor Leavitt either. You were the first I saw."

Ruth looked around, still trying to recover her mental balance. The ground was brick hard and strewn with gravel. Her cuts and scrapes began to smart, but she knew that she'd been fortunate. The accident was catastrophic. "Are you all right, Fenton?" She touched the young man's face. His cheekbone was bruised and his clothes caked with sand, but he brushed off her concern.

"I flew right out of the carriage and landed on the soft bank up above. I think I've been spared any noticeable injury, thank the Lord." He looked about at the scattered wreckage, heard the whining horses, and paused. "I'm a bit stunned," he conceded.

Ruth was on her feet but still struggling for balance. "Lucie!" she screamed hoarsely. "Are you all right? Lucie, where are you?"

Fenton helped steady her as she continued to look about. The scene was frightening. The passenger compartments of the carriage lay sideways at the bottom of the wash, their leather covers peeled back and their wooden panels cracked. Both doors were split open. The compartments had broken away, seats and all, from the wagon underneath, a wagon which was now upside down in the gully, its large wheels freakishly rolling in the air. The rough sideways plunge down the bank had also spilled much of the freight; the goods that remained were enough to lift the wagon inches off the ground—the bundle of hides, the barrel of salt, the crate of farm implements, and Sister Cottam's quilts. Some of the freight was heavy enough not to scatter, although the salt barrel had broken open, spreading its contents around like frost. A lone horse tromped unsteadily through the wreckage in the wash. Two others, still dragging the harness, limped about the broken road above. The fourth, for the moment, had disappeared.

Ruth pushed herself toward the upturned wagon, still calling Lucie's name. Fenton followed, his hand on her back, his eyes roving the top of the gully and beyond. Where was Tom? He should be here, taking charge and cursing their misfortune.

Just then, Ruth threw her hand to her mouth and gasped, and Fenton forgot about Tom. There was Lucie lying up to her shoulders and barely visible beneath the wagon and its scattered freight. Frantically, Ruth and Fenton shoved away the debris and shouted the girl's name. She was pinned from the waist down and covered up to her shoulders, the heavy wagon and its contents smothering her.

Ruth fell to her knees and crawled toward the young woman while Fenton began throwing out loose items that had been wedged around her.

"Lucie, dear girl, we're here," she cried. "We're here." She touched Lucie's cheek, saw her eyelids flutter, and noticed blood in her hair and in the grime of her dirty, tearstained face. The girl groaned and made an attempt to move, but she seemed to be locked in a twisted position beneath the wagon. Her blouse was torn, one sleeve ripped completely off her shoulder; sand covered everything, and she began to sputter for breath.

"Don't worry, Lucie," pleaded Ruth. "We're here. We'll help you. You'll be all right." She tried to lift some of the debris, to give the panting girl more room, and though Ruth managed to push some of the bundles away and Fenton worked to form a pocket of space, the wagon itself held tight.

With her one free hand, Lucie suddenly clutched at Ruth's collar in a surge of panic. "I can't move," she cried. "I can't get out!"

Fenton found a full canteen, and Ruth pressed its spout to Lucie's lips. "We'll help you. You'll be all right," she said, dripping a little water on a piece of her own torn dress and wiping the girl's cheeks and forehead. The bloodstains came from an ugly gash just beneath her hairline. Ruth touched it gingerly, but Lucie winced and turned her head, still gasping. "Lucie, Lucie, listen to me." Ruth tried to calm her. "I need to know just where you're hurt. Can you feel your legs? Can you wiggle your toes? What can you move?"

"I don't know," cried Lucie, frantically shaking her head.

"Try," pleaded Ruth. "Try, Lucie. Try to wiggle something."

Lucie was still gripping Ruth's collar, making a futile effort to use it for leverage, trying to pull herself up. She groaned and relaxed her hold. "I can't. I can't," she said and fell back, breathing hard.

"Can you *feel* anything?" asked Fenton over Ruth's shoulder.

"I think I'm bleeding," said Lucie. "It's wet and warm. The pain is dreadful. But I can't move. There's some heavy weight crushing my legs." Trembling uncontrollably, she grabbed Ruth's hand again. "Sister Fox! Please help me. Get me home!"

Fenton continued tearing out anything loose from around Lucie until only the bulk of the wagon itself remained on top of her. Ruth held her and with soothing words tried to calm her terror. "I *will* get you home, Lucie," she whispered in the girl's ear. "I will get you home."

The panic gradually eased, and Lucie lay back, her large eyes filled with tears. "My leg is throbbing," she murmured. "I can hardly bear it, but I can feel it now."

Ruth patted the girl's cheek and held her, running gentle fingers through her hair. "Try to calm yourself," she whispered. "Try to ease yourself away from panic. God will help you stand the pain. He is with you, Lucie. None of us will leave you. You're going to be all right." Lucie seemed to relax as Ruth's soothing words continued. Shortly after, she eased into semiconsciousness, escaping the agony at hand.

Ruth and Fenton crawled out from under the debris and stood looking hopelessly at each other. They walked a little ways, circling in their tracks and speaking in whispers. They joined hands and said a prayer, and Ruth felt strengthened by it. Fenton remained uncertain and confused about what to do for Lucie.

"Where is Tom?" he pleaded. "We need to look for him. He must be hurt or dazed somewhere up the bank."

Ruth's wrenched shoulder was throbbing. She imagined blood, lacerations, and bruises on her legs and upper arms, and her shoulder and ribs were tender to the touch. But she was far more concerned for Lucie than herself. She hated straying very far from the girl, but Fenton seemed dependent on her too. She watched him anxiously as he circled about as if waiting for directions.

"We need Leavitt," he kept repeating. "I don't think I can move that wagon by myself."

"Perhaps the two of us . . ." Ruth offered.

"You're injured, Sister Fox," Meade replied delicately. "And the both of us together don't carry Leavitt's weight." His head dropped.

He was a clerk, a dandy in a suit and tie; the situation caused him shame.

"You go see if you can find Tom," said Ruth gently. "We need to know what's happened to him, how badly he's hurt, before we decide what to do. I'll stay here with Lucie."

"How long can she last . . . like that?" Meade looked sadly, reluctantly, toward the wagon.

"I don't know. I can't tell how badly she's hurt." Ruth flinched at her own words and turned her eyes away. "There is some urgency, I would imagine." She found Fenton's face again and knew he understood.

"I'll go look for Leavitt," the clerk finally decided. "I can do that much on my own."

Ruth watched Fenton turn and scramble up the side of the ravine to what was left of the road above. Fresh anxiety took hold, for she had been so focused on poor Lucie that Tom's fate had been secondary. Now she shuddered, realizing that his failure to appear, to come striding down into the wash cursing their misfortune and putting "his shoulder to the wheel" to save them, did not bode well at all. His injuries were probably serious, and he would be unable to help Lucie.

Ruth limped back to the wagon, glancing several times toward the bank, hoping to see Fenton or hear him calling. The red sun was dipping into the clouds on the far horizon, and the vast desert looked gloomy. Each way Ruth turned were cliffs and brush and drifting sand. She ached from her own bruises and lacerations, but she forced the pain from her mind. There was no time to worry over it.

She knelt beside Lucie once again and found the girl stirring. Her cheeks were warm and feverish, and her breath was coming in short gasps. Ruth held the pretty face in her hands and prayed in urgent whispers that only God could hear. She felt Lucie's grip on her arm, and her heart swelled. She had come on this journey to help nurture and save the young women of the Church, and here was one of them. Suddenly she was awash with emotion and more fully aware of her calling than ever before. She kissed the girl's tearstained cheek and wept. "God will take care of you, Lucie, and so will I."

The desert was hot and isolated, offering no forgiveness for whatever mistake had sent them crashing into the gully. Still lightheaded,

Ruth let her mind wander to her Salt Lake City home and the familiar images there. She loved the eastside avenues; the busy thoroughfares filled with wagons, buggies, and motor cars; the university on the hill; the canyons with their rushing streams; and the mountains rising like a fortress. She thought of her children, some in their twenties now, grown up and on their own. Ruth imagined them all, but her thoughts fell most to Lucy Beryl, her thirteen-year-old. She was several years younger than this Lucie. Perhaps because their names were alike, Lucy's face flashed into Ruth's mind most vividly. She saw her own Lucy in this Lucie's image, and, try as she might, Ruth could not sever the connection. "Oh, my girl, my child," she cried inside, feeling as though her own daughter were suffering in the gritty bed underneath the wagon.

"Sister Ruth, please, you've got to come. I've found Leavitt." It was Fenton from the top of the ravine. His words jolted her out of her trance. "Please, please hurry!"

Ruth scrambled up, patting Lucie as she left, hoping the girl couldn't hear the terror in Fenton's voice. She struggled up the side of the gully and saw that he was shaking. "I found Leavitt," he repeated and said nothing more, keeping his eyes away from hers, as he guided her along with his hand on her shoulder. High on the left side of the trail, caught between the limbs and boulders, lay the driver's body, crumpled and twisted in repose. His trail-worn hat still covered part of his face, and the breeze still feathered the tufts of his beard as he lay in the sand, eyes closed, gnarled hands at rest.

Ruth's hand flew to her mouth at first sight of him. She fell to her knees to feel his throat and wrist for any sign of life, and her face twisted into agony. "Oh, Tom," she moaned.

"I think he must have struck his head straight off," said Fenton, looking about. "See how the rocks are sharp and blemished here. It may be blood, Sister Fox, and his head is badly wounded. He probably felt no pain, just went off the buckboard when it bounced, just as you did on the other side."

Ruth put her hands to her face and wept. Poor Tom Leavitt, a man who lived in a country that had "too much grit for civilized people" and found beauty in it just the same. "He stood up to that stranger like a man possessed," whispered Ruth after a moment. "His last words to me were about sacred things. Women and the gospel—they softened him."

"You've got to get back to Lucie," said Fenton, taking her hand to pull her up. "You go along, and I'll take care of things here." When she looked at him quizzically, he added, "I'm going to place Tom out straight. I'll get a blanket from the freight to wrap over him, and as soon as we get to Modena, we'll send someone back." Crisis and the reality of death seemed to be energizing Fenton even as they sobered him.

Turning from Tom's body and looking about, Ruth shuddered. Just beyond the cedars where the driver had first lost control was a makeshift barricade. A dozen tangled tree limbs were stacked helter-skelter across the path and were held down by rocks obviously rolled in to anchor them. Already trembling over finding Tom dead, Ruth's heart began to pound. "The wreck was no accident, Fenton," she said grimly. "Look at this. Someone piled up these rocks and limbs to stop us."

Fenton left Tom's body and moved with Ruth along the crude barricade. For a moment he was speechless. "Looks to be manmade, all right." He stared at Ruth with fresh terror in his eyes. "It's that fellow after Lucie, isn't it? He set this whole thing up."

"We've got to find the rifle right away," Ruth answered, trying to avoid a welling panic, if only for Fenton's sake. His hands were shaking as he worked to push some of the limbs out of their path.

Moving past Tom's body, Ruth took a final look at the good man lying there, and tears filled her eyes again. She rolled his shoulder gently and found the matchbook in his pocket. Putting it in her own, she turned toward the task at hand—survival.

The sight of Tom weighed on Ruth like few things in her life. She stooped under its reality and was physically weakened by it. Now she cherished the few moments she had bounced along beside him on the wagon seat. He had enjoyed her company. Even then she sensed as much, and she was glad now that she'd taken the opportunity to share it. Good Tom Leavitt dead! She would not tell Lucie, she decided, at least not now. Nor would she mention the man-made pile of rocks and branches. Lucie had enough to deal with.

The girl's face was wet with tears and perspiration when Ruth returned, and she was in obvious distress. "I want my mother," she murmured. "I want my mother!"

"She's far away, Lucie," Ruth whispered, "and I'm here in her place. We both need to summon the courage to see her prayers are answered. You'll do that for me, won't you, Lucie? You'll stay strong for me, as you would for her."

The words seemed to invigorate Lucie, and she began to talk furiously as if speech could ease the pain. "It was nothing at first, Sister Fox. I couldn't even feel it. Then it tingled, like when you hit your elbow the wrong way. And now it burns, as if I'm lying in a fire pit." She said all this in short gasps, moaning quietly when Ruth gave her water and tried to comfort her.

"Drink this. Keep the thirst away. We'll rig up something to shade your face until we can get you out." Tom's fate and finding the barricade had jolted Ruth, and now she faced a new and searing fear, but she kept that anxiety from Lucie, offering only encouragement and hope. Desperately, she began searching the wreckage for the Henry rifle and found it under what remained of the splintered buckboard railing. Lifting it to get the feel of its weight again, Ruth closed one eye and checked its aim. She hadn't handled a gun with serious purpose in years, but she vowed not to let go of this one.

Ten minutes later, Fenton appeared, and together they tried to make Lucie as comfortable as possible. Then they backed away from her a little to whisper quietly. "You must use your priesthood, Fenton," Ruth told the young man. "This girl needs a blessing."

"I don't know if I can," returned Meade. "I never . . . well, I never really have . . . blessed anyone."

"You blessed your baby, didn't you?" said Ruth. "You've prayed. You've blessed the sacrament."

Meade nodded uncomfortably. His baby hadn't been trapped under a wagon. The sacrament involved a standard prayer he had learned by rote.

"Just pray from your heart," Ruth urged, whispering. "Just bless her that her pain might be eased until we can find a way to free her. I don't know how long she can suffer and still survive. She needs what you have to give."

Together, Ruth and Fenton knelt at Lucie's side. He laid his hands upon her head. He prayed beautifully, filled with a power that he didn't know he had, and when he stood again, he felt humbly satisfied with what he'd done. Ruth continued to hold the girl, rocking her, soothing her, until she was able to relax again and breathe more easily. Ruth murmured a song and encouraged Lucie to be brave. God was with her and so were they. And all the while, Ruth kept the Henry rifle close at hand and remained alert for any unwelcome sound in the ravaged gully.

***

The late afternoon sun dipped below the edge of the ravine, affording shade for Lucie. With two long pieces of the damaged carriage, Fenton assembled an awning above her head, using the buggy tarp as cover. Dust swirled up and down the wash with every movement of the wandering horses, two of which Fenton tethered to the wreckage. The others had found their way into the gully and now looked on, snorting with questioning interest, stepping gingerly. The carriage had belonged to them, and they were reluctant to leave the scene, having heard no familiar driver's voice.

Fenton, too, looked about continually, anxiously. His spectacles had been lost, and he squinted hard without them. Ruth watched him sympathetically. He was so young, just a boy in many ways. He wiped his eyes and mouth with his handkerchief. "What'll we do?" he asked after tethering the horses. "It was Tom who knew the country."

Ruth motioned toward the upturned wheels of the carriage. "Leavitt's gone," she said. "He can't help us now. But you and I have to do what we can for Lucie. Let's make a try with the wagon." Taking Fenton by the arm, she moved through the debris. They pushed trunks and barrels out of the way and found the edge of the wagon box perpendicular to where Lucie lay. Ruth longed for Tom's bulk and strength. Not only were she and Fenton puny in comparison, but Lucie needed her; she could have wrapped her arms around the girl while the men lifted the wagon. Now she was afraid that she and Fenton would lose their grip and drop it before poor Lucie could be moved.

But what if Lucie was worse off than they imagined? Ruth guessed that at least one of Lucie's legs was broken, perhaps crushed. There were doubtless other injuries as well, and Ruth feared underestimating the extent of the damage, which would make movement dangerous for Lucie. The risk came clearly to Ruth as she and Fenton attempted to get a grip on the edge of the wagon and realized for the first time just how heavy it was. Putting every ounce of strength they had into the effort, they were able to barely lift it, and when they were forced to carefully set it back again, Lucie's groan sent a chill through both of them.

"We have to lift the entire wagon and roll it over all at once." Ruth was breathless as she spoke. "We can't chance just lifting it and maybe letting it fall back."

Fenton shook his head. "It's a lot of weight, too much to flip over."

"We've got to try, Fenton! We've got to try!" Ruth was frustrated. She was accustomed to solving problems, getting things done. Here was a crisis, and she would not be constrained. "What about the horses?" she cried. "Could we somehow use them to pull the weight? Or could we take the wheels off? That would surely lighten it."

"We've got no tools," Meade answered hoarsely. "The horses could pull the wagon, maybe, but not as carefully as we need. Might do more harm than good."

He looked at the wagon edge again and back at Lucie. Feeling helpless and inadequate, he made another effort at lifting the box, and Ruth leaned forward to help, but it was no use. They tried again, Fenton lifting the edge by inches, as Ruth caught Lucie under her shoulders and attempted to pull her out while the edge was raised. But the girl screamed and begged Ruth not to move her. She was wedged in too tight to force the issue, and Fenton finally eased his grip again. This time they saved further injury to Lucie by shoving the thick silverware case, Lucie's wedding silver, under the edge, keeping the wagon a few more inches off the ground, but the problem remained. Lucie was still trapped, and Ruth could do nothing but hold her in her arms, kiss her cheeks, and dry her tears.

Chapter Three

DESPERATE MEASURES

Darkness came like a shadow to the gully. So intent were Ruth and Fenton on their work, they almost failed to notice the last light slipping away. Suddenly there was a full moon watching them—a stalker's moon, pale and bright against the sky. It made the little encampment of wreckage easy to see in spite of the blackness around them. One of the loose horses wandered forlornly in the midst of the debris, stepping noisily, its hoof crushing a hatbox in its path. Ruth gathered up pieces of cardboard and asked Fenton to find enough wood to build a fire downwind from the wagon. She knew well the chill of the prairie after sundown and was grateful she'd remembered Leavitt's matches. They wrapped one of Sister Cottam's quilts around Lucie's shoulders, bundling her the best they could. Lucie groaned less constantly now, too weak and tired to complain. Her listlessness worried Ruth. She would sooner have had the girl awake and alert in spite of the pain.

Once the fire was well fed, Ruth made a torch by winding a piece of her petticoat around the end of a long broken carriage brace. Its paint fueled the flame until the cloth caught hold. She drove the torch in the ground near Lucie so she could watch the girl through the night, hoping that the torch and the larger fire weren't guiding trouble to the gully. No one had appeared, but Ruth and Fenton were wary there in the shadows, and each kept one ear cocked.

Ruth examined the Henry by the torch's light. Throwing the lever, she ejected five shells and checked the breach to make certain the barrel was empty. She hesitated a moment, looking at the bullets in her hand. A humorless smile crossed her lips. What would the sisters at home think if they could see her now? Ruth May Fox, poet, YLMIA leader, honored mother in Zion. And here she was, thinking about jacking a cartridge into the barrel of a Henry .44 in the desert. Her dormant skill with the rifle, however, suddenly came to life and brought back memories of her father on the plains.

Almost forty years before, he had shown her how to load and shoot a gun like this. "This lever all the way down," he said, "jacks a bullet in the barrel. And each time you pull the trigger and throw the lever, it jacks another in, this way. By pushing the lever forward when you're finished, you can eject the shells. Look in the breach as well to see if there's a cartridge left in the barrel. You can see the back end of the bullet if you peek down the barrel just right. Sometimes folks forget about that one, that last bullet in the barrel—or the pipe, we sometimes call it. Always check. Never leave one in the pipe if you're done shooting. It's a dangerous thing to think your gun is empty when it's not. And don't jack one in the barrel at all unless you're ready to shoot or know you soon will be. 'Course it's best to be prepared if you figure trouble's comin'. Just ease the hammer down if you're keepin' a bullet there. Don't leave the rifle cocked."

Forty years. Ruth had not handled a Henry more than once or twice in all that time, but she remembered her father's words to her and thought of him as she hefted the heavy rifle now. Could she, a respected woman of the Church, ever actually use this weapon? Could she shoot anything—or anyone? The stranger's growl came into her ears. "*I want the girl! Leave her behind, and the rest of you can move on.*" Ruth thought of Lucie lying helpless under the wagon. She looked into the darkness around her. Carefully, she reloaded the five shells, jacking one of them into the barrel.

When Ruth returned to the fire, she had made up her mind. "You'll have to pick out one of the horses and ride to Modena at first light," she told Fenton. "Someone needs to go for help, and I can't leave Lucie." She looked into the flames as he fidgeted reluctantly beside her. "You can ride bareback. Just squeeze with your knees and hold on to the mane. The horse, more than likely, will follow the road, so you won't need a bit and bridle."

Fenton's face was red in the firelight. He nodded, but there was no eagerness in him. "I'll do it," he said, "but I don't know if it's best."

"Lucie's in a bad way. We can't wait here for help to come out of nowhere or for that stranger to come back."

"And suppose he does," said Fenton. "I don't like leaving you alone."

"It's what we need to do," declared Ruth firmly. She lifted the Henry and watched its breach glint in the reflection of the fire. "We'll be all right," she said.

There was a long pause. Ruth wasn't really sure if Fenton was more afraid to be alone on the trail or to leave her. She looked at him then took his arm, and together they prayed, as they'd always done before each section of their journey. Ruth wanted to let the young man be the voice, but he deferred to her. He held the priesthood, but she was "senior" here. Though her humble words were full of pleading, they were full of faith as well, and both Ruth and Fenton were filled with confidence and the comforting Spirit of the Lord.

"First light, then," Fenton said when Ruth had finished, and he slowly went to tie up the wandering horse that was close by. It was a bit smaller than the others and perhaps easier to mount.

Ruth didn't sleep. Her back ached; her shoulder throbbed. Dried blood still traced her scalp and marked a path behind her ear. She curled up in one of Sister Cottam's quilts and lay near Lucie, one hand on the girl's arm, the other on the Henry .44 beneath the blanket. Lucie often woke up weeping during the night, and each time she moaned, Ruth whispered to her and let her murmur her fears.

"Albert will be so worried," Lucie whispered and then repeated her fiancé's name. "Albert, Albert, Albert," and Ruth ached for her.

Dozing a little, Ruth was haunted by fleeting images: Tom Leavitt, bold and cheerful on the buckboard seat; her father, James, toting the Henry rifle; her husband, Jesse, smiling in his Sunday suit. Most of all, she seemed to dream of her own Lucy Beryl, thirteen years old and chasing the dog around the house, her single braid flying behind her. Odd, what dreams come in the midst of crisis.

***

The sky was just softening into pearl gray when Ruth opened her eyes. The sun wasn't yet up, and the ground was cold beneath her. She immediately turned to Lucie and found her pale, cold, and breathing uneasily. Ruth wrapped the girl's quilt more tightly around her. Lucie murmured but continued to sleep, and Ruth silently said another prayer before painfully rising to join Fenton a few yards down the gully where he'd staked the horse. He'd found a bit of rope and looped it over the animal's ears; he smiled weakly at Ruth's approach. The gully's bed was littered with sharp stones, and she carried the gun, stumbling as she walked, looking nervously about for any sign of unwanted company. Fenton watched her pause, take off her buttoned shoe, and slam it on the nearest rock to break the heel. She followed with the other shoe and was left with two flat soles, thin and fragile though they were. Seeing Fenton watching her, she managed a smile. Her own wounds ached dully now, and she was stiff and sore, but there was some hope in the fact that it was morning and the stranger had not arrived.

"I haven't ridden much," Fenton admitted as Ruth approached, "at least not without a saddle. I've been up most the night thinking about it." Ruth believed him. He was haggard and unshaven; his clothes were torn and covered with sand. He was no longer the dapper clerk Ruth knew. He looked around at the gray light beginning to fill in the shadows. "I guess it's time to take a dare."

"You'll be fine," said Ruth.

Fenton fished a pocket piece out of his vest. "My watch says it's just after five. I hope to make Modena in a couple of hours at the most, maybe sooner if I can hang on when he gallops." He smiled a little sheepishly. "I'm no farm boy, Ruth. I never was."

"You'll be all right, Fenton. Really, there's not that much to riding a horse."

"What about you . . . and the girl?" Fenton was as sober as she'd ever seen him. "Will *you* be all right?"

Ruth felt the depth of his concern. She was his responsibility, after all. "There's no other way," she said. "We'll be all right."

"A man's not supposed to leave you," Fenton reminded her, thinking of the rules that governed her journeys for the Church.

Ruth lifted the rifle, patting the barrel. "Henry's here," she said with a twinkle, and Fenton smiled, suddenly loving Ruth May Fox with the emotion of an adoring son.

After several minutes, Fenton found a box to stand on, and Ruth held the horse as he struggled awkwardly onto its back. The animal stomped and snorted and turned in a circle and tossed its head, unfamiliar with the rider. But Fenton soon found his grip. Ruth led the horse up the gully to a soft, shallow place to mount the bank. She gave Fenton one of the canteens and the end of the rope, and both of them prodded the horse, which finally struggled through the sand to the road above. They had already passed the barrier, and as the clear trail lay before him, Fenton was confident enough to turn and wave back at Ruth . . . until the horse suddenly found its stride and began to sprint down the familiar road with the little clerk clinging desperately to the rope and the pony's shaggy mane.

"Heyyyy!" Fenton screeched, and the word was finally lost in the distance, along with the sound of the horse's gallop.

Ruth watched Fenton until he disappeared, but her soft smile turned sour as she retraced her steps back down the gully toward the wreckage. The sun was creeping up on the eastern horizon between ribbons of pink clouds, but it was still chilly enough to need a fire. Ruth stirred the glowing coals and managed to coax another flame, feeding it with kindling from the broken carriage. Hunger gnawed at her, and she remembered that poor Fenton had left without any breakfast, if there was any to be had. They had been too preoccupied to think about food the night before, but now she was weak, still hurting from her injuries and lightheaded. She knew that Lucie needed nourishment as well. Once again, she searched through the scattered bags and boxes, finding some hardtack in Tom's pouch. The basket where their lunch had been packed was crushed, but two chipped beef sandwiches were still inside, flattened but still edible. The second canteen was still half full.

Ruth nestled beside Lucie, who woke up grimacing. The young woman would sip water only at Ruth's insistence. Lucie turned her face away from the bread and its odor until Ruth again encouraged her. "You must keep up your strength. You must try, Lucie. You must eat, even just a little bit."

Lucie finally swallowed a bite or two and took a little water. She was wan and listless. "I think I fainted during the night," she muttered. "I might have, Sister Fox. I might have even died and then come back because Albert prayed for me. I might have stayed dead if it weren't for that."

"You're not going to die, Lucie," said Ruth firmly, "not here, not now."

Lucie's eyes were suddenly wide and frightened, and Ruth prayed fervently as she watched the girl struggle. "Brother Meade has gone to Modena on one of the horses. He'll bring help, maybe in just a few hours. Hang on," she added as Lucie gripped her wrist. "Hang on to me."

Later, when Lucie was quiet again and the sun was full and blazing, Ruth lay beside the girl under the shade of the tarp. There seemed but little else to do. Keep Lucie calm and as comfortable as possible. Keep herself alert and out of the swelling heat. They talked then, the young bride-to-be and this national activist mother of twelve. "Do you believe in premonitions, Sister Fox?" whispered Lucie, suddenly growing stoic again. "I mean, perhaps we're warned of our troubles ahead of time, but we don't bother to listen."

"What do you mean, Lucie?"

"I mean that when I told you I didn't know the man on the road, that wasn't quite the truth."

"Did you know him?" Ruth was shocked and sat up, looking squarely into Lucie's eyes. "Did you really know who he was?"

"No, but I felt I did." Lucie's voice grew husky again, and it was hard for her to speak. "For the past few weeks, I've been haunted by the notion that someone was watching me. On the street, in the yard at school, sometimes even at church. I'd look around and no one was there, but I felt him, his eyes, his smell . . . like when you know that someone's in a dark room but you can't see them until the lights come on."

"Lucie, did you mention this to anyone?"

"No. I thought it was all in my mind, that I was only anxious about the wedding. But, honestly, looking back, there seemed to be somebody there."

"And you think it's the same man who stopped us on the road?"

"I don't know, but maybe the haunting was a sign to me that I shouldn't take this route or make this trip or . . ." Lucie's eyes welled up. " Or marry Albert!"

"Now, you listen to me," said Ruth, clasping the girl's hand. "I won't have you blaming yourself for what's happened here, nor the devil either. An evil man has crossed your path, Lucie. Perhaps he has stalked you, become obsessed with you, bided his time until you were isolated and vulnerable. But what he's done has nothing to do with warning signs. And it has nothing to do with Albert. He's waiting for you in Salt Lake, and by my life, you'll get home to him, no matter what some stranger thinks he can do to stop you."

Lucie was suddenly shaking. "Did the stranger cause this wreck?" she cried hoarsely, trying to rise. "Is he coming for me? Oh, no, no, no . . . Albert! Mama! Oh, Sister Fox!"

Ruth bit her tongue. She hadn't intended to tell Lucie about the barricade. "I'm right here," she repeated, holding the girl's head between her hands. "You're going to be all right. Brother Meade has gone for help. He'll be back here very soon." As she spoke, she moved her hands to Lucie's shoulders, trying with gentle force to stop the girl's trembling. The panic finally eased as Ruth murmured softly, and slowly laid Lucie's head back on the makeshift pillow.

Lucie was quiet then, and Ruth was the one who needed calming. She was agitated and worried and began to anxiously watch the road. She believed Lucie's story about someone stalking her. It helped explain things. But it aroused a panic too, one she fought to suppress as she searched the wash with weary eyes and gripped the rifle tightly, praying to God that the rescue party from Modena would arrive before the man in the red bandana.

***

It was high noon when Ruth awakened with a start. Footsteps! Heavy
boots were stomping through the debris. There, alongside Lucie,
Ruth had fallen asleep and now regretted it. She lifted her Henry rifle
and hung back in the shade of the tarp, hoping to catch a glimpse of
the man before he saw her. But it was too late. Soon he was hulking
over her not five feet away. It was indeed the stranger who had
stopped them on the road, with his dark eyes, husky shoulders, and
sullen smile. He looked at Ruth with a contemptuous glare, and then
he stared at Lucie, wetting his lips as he sized up her predicament. It
dawned upon Ruth that the man had been nearby all along, waiting
for the dust to settle, watching to see who had survived. Waiting for
Fenton to leave. Surely, this was more than he had bargained for.
Certainly, he hadn't expected Lucie to be so badly injured or Tom
Leavitt to be killed. A breakdown, perhaps, a missing wheel. That
was all he'd planned. Seeing a different result altogether, he must have
waited through the night until Fenton left for help. Yes, he'd sized up
everything. He'd probably even retraced the road for several miles,
making certain no other travelers were about. Now he put his hands
on his hips and surveyed the damage with some satisfaction, paying
little heed to the woman at Lucie's side or the rifle in her hands.

"Get out of here!" Ruth cried, furiously raising the Henry. "Go
on! Get back! Get back where you came from, or I'll use this gun to
send you there!"

The stranger looked at Ruth as if he hadn't noticed her before.
He stepped back when she waved the gun at him, more amused than
threatened. "What you got there," he said, "a .44? Why, a little thing
like you could hardly cock such a big piece. Ya sure that thing's loaded?
I don't believe it is."

"You want to find out? Come another step, and I'll show you."

"Now, you don't look like a woman who knows guns. You look
like a frilly woman, used to city manners and fine music. Where's
your menfolk? They got nerve, leaving a lady like you alone out here."
The man looked around, eyeing the gully of debris from one end to
the other. "Yer driver sure made a mess of things."

Ruth was on her feet, and with the rifle she prodded him until
he stepped back and raised his hands as if to humor her. "Looks like

the little gal needs help," he said, spitting tobacco juice. "How long can she last under that there wagon? Yep, yer driver made a mess of things. He shoulda turned over that girl to me yesterday and not caused all this trouble."

"Are you insane?" cried Ruth, leveling the rifle. "No one is going to let you touch that girl. Especially me!"

The stranger looked around her shoulder at Lucie. Then his smile faded, and he scowled at Ruth. "Who are you, anyway?" he spit. "You her ma?"

"No, but I'll pull this trigger just the same."

"You've got a flair about you," sneered the man, "a fancy way of holding yourself, like you're some kind of high and mighty. You're tiny though. Why, without that .44, I could twist you like taffy candy, and I'd do it too."

Ruth held the rifle steady. Her eyes flashed at the man though her heart was pounding. He was grimy and wet with perspiration, smarmy in his manner and speech, and bullish in his stance. The red scarf looked so out of place around his neck that Ruth guessed he'd stolen it. She saw brutality in his hands, in the sullen way he curled his lip, and in the cocksure tilt of his chin. "Go on, get out of here," she demanded once again, gesturing with the barrel. "Help is coming from Modena. You'll have the devil to pay if they find you here."

The stranger laughed. "Modena?" he cried. "There ain't nobody in Modena but a sorry old station clerk and a herd of goats. Ha! Modena. There's nobody there can help that girl, nor you either, fancy lady."

"What do you want with us? Why are you doing this?" raged Ruth in desperation. "A good man is dead because of you!"

The stranger spit again and shrugged. He nodded toward the over-turned wagon. "I've had my eye on that little gal there for a while now. My woman died last winter. There wasn't no women around here, so God sent me to town and showed me Lucie there. Yeah, I know her name. I know a lot about her. I used to watch her when she went to school and to church. I brushed right by her once when she was in the mercantile store. I smelt her perfume that day and ain't never forgot the bloom of it." He paused, as if remembering, then his tongue sharp-ened. "She's the one God means for me to have, and no one's gonna stop me from gettin' her. It warn't my plan to have yer driver die, but that was his concern, not mine. It warn't my plan to have Lucie hurt like this, but maybe that's God's doin' too. It'll take a lot of healin', I 'spect, 'fore she can run away, and by that time she'll be used to me and be my wife."

Ruth was livid. She sprang at the man and jerked the barrel of the gun, leveling it at his chest. "You get out of here before I put a bullet through your black heart, you piece of human filth! You come around here again, and so help me, I'll forget my principles. Go on, get out!" She waved the Henry at him and forced him back, prodding him with the barrel until he moved some distance away, still chuckling to himself and watching her with cold and narrow eyes.

"I'm leavin'," he finally cackled. "I'm goin' up the wash a ways. You can wait for the pip-squeak ya sent to Modena to come back, if you think he will, but I'm bettin' you'll fall dead asleep, with yer gun beside you, before him or anyone else ever shows up here." The man was still laughing as he turned his back, trudging up the gully, while Ruth, in a cold sweat, watched him go. He did not look at her again and paused only to occasionally squirt tobacco juice and kick the sand with his boots. He was gone before Ruth stopped trembling.

She hurried back to Lucie, worried over how much the girl had heard, numbed by the reality she faced. Had Lucie seen the stranger? Ruth found the girl ghostlike and only semiconscious. She had fainted once again. Ruth pressed water to Lucie's lips, ran her fingers through the girl's hair, and kissed her cheeks, but Lucie was unresponsive. Pain had done its work. With no real nourishment, no treatment for her wounds, and no relief from her entrapment, Lucie had receded into a life-threatening exhaustion that left her listless and glassy-eyed.

Ruth was panic-stricken. Desperately she prayed. "Lucie, you've got to stay with me. You've got to hang on." Lucie barely moved, but her eyelids fluttered and gave Ruth some hope. Finally, the woman lay down beside the girl as a mother would. Keeping the rifle close, she nevertheless forced all thought of danger from her mind and tried to whisper encouragement in Lucie's ear. What could she say? What blessing could she pronounce? An evil man stood waiting, his footprints in the sand leading up the gully and out of sight. She and the Henry rifle were all that stood between him and this helpless girl.

What could she possibly do? The man was right. She was hungry, wounded, and physically exhausted. She would undoubtedly fall asleep before Fenton returned, if he did at all. But Ruth May Fox was no weakling in spirit. She prayed with every ounce of faith she had and spoke afterward to Lucie with a whisper. "You will survive, my darling. You will survive. God will tell me how to save you, and I will. For all the miles I've traveled, for all the women I've reached, I can't lose you. To me, you are another Lucy Beryl, and I will die for you as I would for her."

***

Throughout the rest of the long day, Ruth waited. Against the sky, the sun rolled like a glowing coal in clouds of white ash. The heat was blistering outside the cover of the tarp. Ruth feared the return of the stranger and kept her fingers on the rifle beside her. She feared a sudden summer shower too, and the clouds were a threatening omen. The gully was surely vulnerable to flash flooding. As the air grew humid, Ruth brooded over that possible disaster. She remained at Lucie's side, listening to the rhythm of her breath, whispering encouragement whenever the girl stirred, and praying for the sound of wagons and horses on the Modena trail. But she heard only the crickets and insects of the desert, the screech of a bird, the call of a distant coyote or wolf. She saw a hawk soaring lazily in the sky and wondered about buzzards being drawn to Tom's body; although, thankfully, none appeared. When she briefly stood to check the gully and the road, all was quiet. The only sign of the stranger was a curl of gray smoke lifting gently near a patch of sagebrush half a mile down the wash. He wasn't far away.

The wilderness is such a paradox, Ruth mused, *beautiful and deadly all at once. Natural with all its mysteries but spiritual in its influence on the soul.* The isolation of the desert was frightening, as the plains had been when she'd first crossed them. She remembered the vast, wind-swept prairie, as endless as an ocean, with nothing to mark a friendly crossroads or a destination. Nothing. And yet, and yet their journey had traced a trail where thousands had passed before and thousands would still. The land would be good to them and give of itself, and they would treasure its abundance. Perhaps there was some similar answer here. Somehow she had to find it.

Toward evening, Lucie stirred a little, and Ruth gave her water and tried to make her suck on the last of the crackers. She refused, having no strength to chew and no interest in food. Ruth sang to her again, softly, gently, a familiar tune, and Lucie managed a wan smile before her eyes rolled back. Alarm filled Ruth again, and she shook the girl and cried out her name. Lucie's breath came in weak and weary gasps. When she seemed to relax and breathe more evenly, Ruth's panic continued, for Lucie's resolve seemed to be fading. Ruth stared at her, fearing they were losing this desperate struggle so crucial for them both.

Suddenly, Ruth answered an urge to stand and climb up to the road. There she squinted toward the north for any sign of horses or riders. There was nothing, only a leaden sky and a vista of sand dotted by clumps of sage and hedgehog cactus. It wasn't going to rain, but the air would chill, as usual, leaving the gully cold and dark.

Ruth turned back to the wagon, desperate and alone. On her knees again at Lucie's side, she prayed, pleading with the Lord for guidance. A warm glow swelled within her, which at first left her confused. Then she was struck with an affirmation she could not deny. But even as she rose up, feeling God had spoken, she hesitated, trying to gather courage for what she was about to do.

***

First, she built the fire up again, adding sticks and paper and the ruined hatbox pieces, but her mind remained on the smoke at the other end of the gully. She could easily pick out the stranger's camp several hundred yards away. She could smell the smoke and even the meat sizzling in the coals, perhaps a bird the man had killed and skewered on a stick. The flame was bright, licking and snapping in the shadows. It was his signal, tempting her to yield, capitulate, raise the white flag of surrender, save pretty Lucie's life. She knew he was waiting. Still, she lingered until the night was like pitch and Fenton's return with help was utterly impossible. Then, she gathered up the Henry rifle and trudged wearily up the wash toward the light.

The stranger rose from his haunches as she approached, curling his lips into that same grim smile. The reflection of the firelight on his jowls and whiskers made him appear demon-like and licentious, even without his threats, and Ruth was careful to keep her weapon aimed. "So your posse never showed," he said scornfully.

"I need your help." Ruth was stiff and firm, and her fingers tightened on the rifle as she spoke. "Lucie is dying. You're going to lift that wagon off her, or I swear I'll kill you where you stand."

"Whoa!" The stranger's hands flew up in mock excitement. "Ya don't have to shoot me. Saving that gal is what I've wanted all along. I'd have done it this mornin' if ya hadn't drove me away."

"You'll do it now."

She gestured with the gun for him to rise and move ahead of her and made a point of staying past his reach. He did as she demanded, though he took his time, stretching and unfolding his legs as if it were a great effort to even move. When Ruth prodded him, he walked slowly, frequently casting a sly glance over his shoulder, forcing her to push him along with the barrel of the gun.

"How long you gonna keep that Henry aimed at me?" he chortled once. "It's dang near big as you. I ain't sure but what it might go off. Then who would save poor Lucie?"

"Just walk," demanded Ruth, "and be quick about it."

The moonlight blanketed the gully, and Ruth's fire blazed ahead of them. At the overturned wagon, the man paused then walked about, assessing the challenge of lifting it. When he came to where Lucie lay listless, Ruth moved in front of her, brandishing the Henry.

"You just tend to the wagon," Ruth snapped. "That's all I want from you."

The man eyed the girl and took some pleasure in it. "She is a pretty little thing," he muttered. "I *have* liked watching her."

Repulsed, Ruth gestured with the gun. "Go on. Get to your work. You can see what you need to do."

The man smiled mockingly and moved to the place where Ruth and Fenton had tried to lift the wagon. "I can see what I need to do, all right," he laughed, "and I can see why that skinny fool with you was as worthless as a shriveled seed."

"Get on with it," prodded Ruth.

Playing with her patience, the stranger casually looked over the wagon again. "I don't know," he said. "This ol' bed is as heavy as a anvil in a quicksand hole. What if I cain't lift it? And what's gonna happen if I do? What's gonna happen then? Yer Lucie's gonna need lookin' after, an' you won't have no extra hands to keep that Henry aimed at me. Fact is, I think it's gettin' wobbly in yer grip already. I've a notion ya haven't slept much in the last two days. Maybe not at all. How long do ya think you kin keep that barrel up, as tired as ya are?"

"Long enough," Ruth snapped. "Now, get on with it."

The man smiled and turned casually to the wagon. Gripping the top edge of one side, he put all of his burly strength into raising it a few inches, pulling it from the dirt where it had settled. Switching the position of his hands, he began an impressive upward push, grunting under the strain. Pieces of the wagon cracked as the weight shifted. Its big wheels squeaked into motion, and the loosened contents of its box crashed noisily into a scattered heap once it was upended. With one last mighty shove, the man tossed the wreckage over, and it fell clattering on its side, well clear of Lucie Cole, who was free at last.

Ruth scrambled to the girl, whose lower body was still covered with heavy baggage. Her left leg—obviously broken—was twisted tightly and awkwardly under the long wooden box of farming implements. Around a ghastly wound between knee and ankle, the misshapen leg was swollen and discolored. The open wound was quickly turning gray. Ruth shuddered. There was little wonder that Lucie had fainted from pain. Ruth whispered to her now, encouraging her, calming her, telling her not to move the leg, as she groaned and rocked in new agony.

Quickly removing everything still in the way, Ruth and her beefy assistant bent to examine Lucie's injuries more closely. The man seemed more interested now in helping than in mocking Ruth and the Henry rifle. But Ruth was still wary. She held Lucie's head in her lap and kept the gun at her side, watching the man as he carefully and methodically worked to straighten the injured leg. "I'd fill 'er with liquor if I had some," he remarked, clenching his teeth as Lucie screamed with every change in the position of her broken bone. Ruth clung to her, holding her down, gripping her flailing arms, and watching the man through her own tears. The fire gleamed on the proceedings, leaving in stark detail the figures in its light—the writhing girl; the stranger working nimbly with the leg; and Ruth, whose piercing eyes had never burned so fiercely.

When the man was satisfied with the way he'd washed the wound and set the bone, he wrapped the leg in flaps of rawhide and bound it tightly with burlap string from the freight, several strands of it up and down the leg. Then, he found stout wooden slats from the wagon and used them to brace each side of the bone, from knee to ankle. He wound these with heavy straps of leather ripped from one of the suitcases. This accomplished, he turned his attention to Lucie's other wounds, lacerations on her right leg and her arms, which he slathered with a prickly pear poultice from his pouch belt. Ruth suspected broken ribs, given Lucie's short gasps of breath, but they could do little for her except wrap muslin tightly around her lower chest. The stranger let Ruth handle this while he looked about for more twine. "Ya shoulda let me have her yesterday," he declared when they had finished and he stood looking at his work. "Woulda saved us all a whole bunch of trouble."

Lucie moaned in Ruth's arms, her face streaked with dust and tears.

The night was as deep as a dark well. The white moon drifted between the shadowy ridges, and from a distance the stranger's fire still shone like a dying coal in the soot of darkness. Lucie, at last too weak to cry, finally settled painfully into sleep, and Ruth May Fox and her companion wearily watched each other as they rested from an unresolved ordeal. *"Ya shoulda let me have her yesterday."* The man's words echoed in Ruth's ears until the shadows of the night engulfed her.

Chapter Four
THE FOLLOWER

RUTH WAS DRAINED OF ENERGY and emotion. The stranger near her slowly became a bleary figure, with only his red bandana clear and sharp in her vision. Sitting next to Lucie, leaning wearily on the long barrel of the gun, she could barely hold her head up. Her hair was frizzled, tufts of it standing here and there in disarray. She was nearly fifty years old, fifty in November, and not as strong as she once was. She dreamed of home and Zion as she mused a little ways from the fire, holding Lucie's head in her lap.

She dizzily watched the dark-faced stranger puttering through the wreckage now, seeing what he could scavenge. He had control of their lives, no doubt. She still had the rifle, but he had the upper hand. She had conceded it to him to save Lucie. She saw as much when his brutish strength lifted the wagon and he had crudely set Lucie's broken leg. She saw it now, as he made his way around the gully, ignoring her and her Henry rifle. He was in charge and he knew it. And what would come of it? What would happen to them, now that evil had command? Her only hope was Fenton and that the help he brought would come in time. *Perhaps by morning, surely by morning . . . It was too dark now, but surely with first light someone would come . . .*

***

Ruth was jerked awake when the rifle was suddenly ripped out of her hand and she heard the stranger's scornful laughter echoing in her ears. She sat up with a start and found him standing over her, hefting the Henry like a new toy. "Lost somethin'?" he said smugly. It was morning, and the light was already hard and full. Ruth rubbed her eyes, reaching for coherence, then instinctively turned to search for Lucie next to her but was terror stricken to see only an empty blanket.

Raising her fists, she rose and sprang wildly at the man, pummeling him and shrieking. "Where is she, you monster? What have you done?"

"Whoa! Whoa!" The man held the rifle crosswise against his chest to fend off Ruth's blows, all the while chortling at the attempts of a tiny woman to attack him. He played with her rage, dodging this way and that, and occasionally snorting, "Oh, ya got me. Ya landed one there." At last he tired of the game. With a hand clutching each end of the rifle, he pushed her solidly across the shoulders, knocking her to the ground with one strong shove. "Settle yourself," he said. "The girl's all right. Come see."

Ruth scrambled after him as he turned up the gully, and there his black horse stood, staked in a widened place where some earlier storm had clawed away the side of the wash. The man had removed his red bandana and hung it on the stick where the horse was tethered as if it were a flag marking some boundary. Behind the horse was a travois the man had assembled, strung between two long limbs of cedar wood. There lay Lucie, wrapped on the stretch of blankets between the poles, looking ill and hopeless. Ruth ran to her, trying to sense Lucie's condition and all that had occurred while she'd been asleep.

The stranger sensed her guilt and toyed with it. "Don't burden yourself, Sister Ruth. Even the Apostles nodded off in the garden when they shoulda been keepin' watch. Remember?"

Ruth was in the man's face again. "How do you know my name?"

"The girl there was callin' for ya." He shrugged. "'Sister Ruth, Sister Ruth,' she said, and sometimes 'Sister Fox,' so I guess that's yer name. Ruth Fox. And I guessed ya was one of them Mormon ladies too, maybe a high-up Mormon lady, since the girl seemed to have that tone." The man smirked condescendingly at her. "Well, I guess ya ought to know *my* name, Sister Ruth. It's Ezra Brackett, but don't put no *brother* on it. You Mormons can't claim me."

"Well, you have my rifle now, Mr. Brackett," Ruth spit back, defiantly. "What do you intend to do with it?"

Brackett looked down at the gun in his hands and smiled. "Why, not a thing," he said. "You kin have it back. I got me a carbine there in the scabbard." With that, he jerked the lever on the Henry and watched the first shell eject then another and another until four bullets had jumped out of the breech.

Ruth made a mental note about the one left in the pipe. Was it still there? There were five before. Five shells. She had counted them. Brackett had ejected only four. She was certain of it. Or was she? It was all a blur, the entire ordeal, and what could she do about it now? She was weak and hungry and ready to imagine anything. Brackett deliberately squinted into the breach and then made a point of menacingly aiming the barrel straight at Ruth.

"I don't see nuthin' in the pipe," he smiled darkly, "but I could be wrong, the way the sun's a-winkin' off the plate." Tauntingly, he cocked the hammer and watched Ruth stiffen in her tracks. "Sometimes it's hard to tell," he teased. "Sometimes you just haff to pull the trigger to find out." He eyed her with a curious glare, waiting to see if she would plead for her life, fall to her knees, beg for mercy. When she did none of these things, he smiled again, a dark, lascivious smile, and finally eased the hammer safely forward with his thumb. "Scared ya, didn't I?" he said, shrugging off her terror.

Ruth exhaled and shot a glance in the direction of the travois. Had she just missed dying on a scoundrel's whim? What would have become of Lucie if Brackett had pulled the trigger, even as a joke? Or, worse, maybe he knew the shell was in the pipe and simply had no compunction about killing her, except that murder was a messy thing and scaring her suited his purpose well enough. Ruth trembled until Brackett suddenly tossed the rifle away as if it were a useless toy. "I got me a carbine," he repeated. "This Henry's too much to carry." He juggled the four ejected bullets in his hand before dropping them in his pocket. "'Course I ain't leavin' a loaded gun for you to plague me with." He winked.

He moved around, patting the horse and checking the frame of the travois and the straps that held it across his saddle. He ignored

Ruth for the most part and only spoke to her as the mood struck him. "I figure someone will come by this way before too long," he told her. "I've got a full water pouch, so I'm leavin' the canteen. I roasted me a tough old buzzard hen last night, but there wasn't much meat on it. What's left is on a stick by my fire. I got no other food to give ya, but like I say, someone is bound to come along."

Ruth had recovered her grit. "Just a moment, Mr. Brackett, if that's indeed your name. Where do you think you're taking Lucie? Into the desert? Into the wilderness where she'll never be found? You *must* be crazy!"

"It's no concern of yours, Sister Ruth," answered Brackett, still fastening the gear. "I'm doin' ya no harm. I got what I come for, and I'm leavin' ya to yer people, healthy and untouched. You kin make it to Modena in an hour once they find ya. Round up one of them carriage horses yerself and get there sooner if ya want. Why, I'm bettin' ya can ride a horse a lot better than that skinny clerk ya sent on a fool's errand. Ha! He ain't never made it back yet, has he? Prob'ly hung up somewhere on a cactus pullin' pricklies out of his toes."

"You're not taking that girl away," cried Ruth, "not without me trailing every mile. You think I'm old and thin and not up to anything because I'm a woman, but I swear to you, as long as I have breath, I won't let her out of my sight."

Brackett stopped his work and looked at her. "Yer bein' crazy, Sister Ruth. This girl's not yer daughter and not even yer kin. It's likely ya got girls at home who need their mama, an' yer gonna die out here in this wild country far away from 'em. An' all fer what? They're yers, and this little gal is mine. God sent me to her. He pointed her out to me. 'She's the one,' He said. Well, I've done His will, even with all this trouble. I've fixed up her busted leg, an' I'm takin' her home with me where she can heal and get to know my people. I've got no reason to harm you. You can sit there under that tarp and wait till your friend comes back, or ya can ride one of these here horses to Modena. But the girl is mine, and I'm takin' her."

"Then I'm going with you," said Ruth, "and you'll have to use that gun to stop me."

Ezra Brackett gave her one last incredulous look and then shrugged his shoulders. "Suit yerself," he spat, "but it's a long way to walk for nuthin'."

Ruth moved to Lucie lying on the crude travois behind Brackett's horse. She bent and kissed the girl's forehead and smoothed her limp, moist hair. "I'll be with you, Lucie," she whispered. "I'm following right behind. I won't lose sight of you."

Lucie squeezed her hand and groaned. "Where . . . ? What's happening? Oh, please, Sister Fox. Help me! Get me home. I want my mother. I want Albert. You've got to get me home!"

Ruth tried to calm her then stepped away, feeling dreadful apprehension for this girl—for both of them. How far was this man taking them? How far could she walk? How long could Lucie suffer? Ruth sized up her options. The two limbs that braced the travois marked a double track in the sand. She would have that track to follow. Brackett would have to move slowly because of the travois, but how long could she keep walking? What about the expected rescue party? How would they find them? Would they see the tracks before the prairie wind covered them? Her mind was racing. She needed something more, something to tell the rescuers where to go. As Brackett puttered with his gear, Ruth searched through the wreckage and found the five-pound barrel split open and spilling salt. Quickly, she scooped up as many handfuls as her pockets would hold and came away proud of her secret in spite of its questionable usefulness.

Furtively, she looked around for anything else she could use. Her eye fell on the crate of tools, and she wondered briefly if a chisel or a twine bolt could help in any way. But the crate was heavy and lying on its top. There was no way to open it without more time than she had. It was hopeless. There was nothing she could take except the salt, for all the use it could be. Then, as she was about to turn away empty-handed, she spied Lucie's little purse lying in the debris. Quickly opening it, Ruth found the silver case with Albert's picture and the little calendar where Lucie marked the days. Slipping the case into her pocket with the salt, Ruth came close to weeping. Life, at times, was extraordinarily cruel.

Brackett suddenly faced her as she emerged from the scattered wreckage. He was holding the Henry again, and his face was cold. Was he only impatient, or had he changed his mind about what he planned to do with her? A wave of fear coursed through Ruth involuntarily. She raised her glistening eyes, hoping the man saw courage there rather than the utter dread she felt. He looked at her, testing her resolve or, perhaps, his own. Finally, he shrugged. With a sudden jerking motion, he tossed the rifle to her, and she threw up her hands to catch it.

"I told ya this was yours," he snarled. "I only got one scabbard, so I ain't got room fer it. But it's a nice rifle. It might serve ya for a walking stick if ya don't mind scratchin' up the stock." He laughed. "Then I'll take it from ya, when you've keeled over in the sand, just to remember ya by. I'll sell it to my brother and know that Sister Ruth carried it for me, dragging it partway home and savin' me the trouble."

"It's not much good unloaded," said Ruth wryly, praying at the same time that she was wrong.

"Well, if ya think I'm gonna give ya back the shells, you ain't as smart as you look." Brackett turned his back. "I'm headed out now. You can stay here or drag that gun along, useless as it is. I ain't givin' ya no mind. You'll never make it far this time of day. I wouldn't be tryin' it myself if I warn't on the run from anyone yer man kin muster up in Modena. But I ain't as skinny as you, either. And, besides, you got a choice."

With those words he walked to his horse, untied it from its stake, and mounted without looking back. The black horse ambled up the gully to a flat gray dune, where Brackett prodded him over a hump of sand where the sharp bank had eroded. Lucie, in her blankets, rolled a little as the travois tipped and bounced on the uneven ground.

Determined, Ruth gathered up her skirt and followed, a canteen of water hanging across her shoulders and her precious salt filling her pockets. The Henry was heavy, but she dragged it along as well. The stray shell in the pipe was all she had to count on—if it was really there—and she clung to the rifle as if it were a lifeline in a storm. The only thing that buoyed her as she moved away from the gully was

Brackett's red bandana still blowing on the stick where he had left it, forgotten in the scattered debris. He had left his mark, and Fenton Meade would recognize it.

Away from the road, well to the west, the desert was a never-ending vista of coarse sand, stone fragments, and clumps of juniper. Rocky mesas, with their flat roofs and rugged walls, rose in the distance like eternal landmarks on a dry oblivion of desolation. Behind them, the nearest mountain range was etched in sharp detail along the horizon, close enough to paint, too far away to promise shade or trees or water. The sky was a dome of vivid blue, and the sun glazed everything with its heat. Brackett was right about the foolishness of daytime travel in this desert. But he was wrong about Ruth's having any choice.

***

Ruth kept pace with the travois for the first two miles as it bumped along on its crooked legs and wedged its tracks into the sand. She tried to keep Lucie's face in view, Lucie's pallid, listless face. How different Lucie was now from the pretty bride-to-be who first boarded the carriage. She had spoken so admiringly of Ruth, calling her "Sister Fox" and looking at her as some kind of celebrity, a rescuer of young women's souls. And here Ruth was, unable to save Lucie without turning her over to this . . . this criminal! What had she done? What had she accomplished? Lucie was no longer trapped under a wagon, but she was hardly better off.

Sadly, Ruth remembered how Lucie had described her mother's plans to celebrate the wedding—music, flowers, food, and laughter. Lucie was obviously a cherished daughter. How could Ruth ever face the Coles if she didn't bring Lucie home? "I love to sing and do theatricals," Lucie had told her. "Albert says he wants me to continue to perform whenever I can and teach our children to do the same. He sees the beauty in it." Now Ruth was struck by the contrast of Lucie's world of charm and grace and loveliness, and the vile wickedness of Ezra Brackett's. It was more than Ruth could bear.

Ruth dragged the Henry by its barrel and thought of the single shell inside. Until now, she hadn't had the chance to check, to squint into the breach and see if the bullet was really there. Certainly Brackett had overlooked it. Perhaps heaven had veiled his eyes. She had loaded five shells. She was sure of it. The vile man was fifty yards ahead, his shoulders sloped, his hat down over his eyes, ignoring the foolish woman who stubbornly trailed him. She could end this crisis with one shot, but having not fired a rifle in forty years, she lacked confidence in her aim, and one chance was all she had. She was also a Saint, a Latter-day Saint. Trudging along in the sand, hungry and spent, she knew she could no more shoot Ezra Brackett in the back than abandon Lucie Cole. Suddenly she didn't want to know if the rifle was still loaded, and for the moment she refused to look.

She thought of discarding the gun. It was heavy and already hard to drag. It would offer her no leverage against Brackett anyway since he thought it wasn't loaded, which was why he was letting her keep it now. Still, the possibility of that single bullet gave her some hope of protection, and in the end she refused to give it up.

The harsh, desolate miles stretched on forever under the burning sun. Brackett and the travois sometimes became no more than a speck in the distance as Ruth was forced to stop at frequent intervals, kneeling under the scant shade of a lone bush or tree and once lying prone in the sparse grass of a dry gully. Her wounds and bruises from the accident had left her stiff and sore and unable to kneel without pain. With small handfuls of salt, she tried to mark the trail at frequent intervals. Like bread crumbs from the storybook, the salt left a clue for any rescuers to follow. She moistened the salt and left it on the stems and thistles of any foliage she passed, but the supply soon diminished and then was gone completely before any crossroads or landmark was reached. She was forced to focus on the route in front of her rather than the one behind, for Fenton's return had become a dream. Ahead lay her challenge, and she pressed on with no other options.

She never entirely lost sight of Brackett's horse and his precious cargo. It was fixed like a dark star in a shimmering ocean of sky and sand. Sometimes Brackett would pause to give water to Lucie and to rest his mount, and Ruth would almost catch up before he climbed into the saddle and moved on again. Once, he stopped and waited, watching her with dull and narrow eyes, tracing her progress as she again approached, dragging the Henry behind her. When she got close enough, he motioned for her to attend to Lucie, and she did so gladly, pressing her own canteen to the girl's lips and then letting water trickle over her face and throat. She pulled the quilts away from Lucie as much as the wrap of the travois would allow and opened up the collar of the girl's dress to help her cool. There was a bit of shade under some pinion trees, and Brackett moved the travois beneath them.

Ruth leaned there exhausted, bending over Lucie. The girl's eyes were red with dust and tears, her bare throat glistened with perspiration. Ruth too was no more the prim and well-groomed matron who had left St. George two days before. She was burned and bruised and dirty; the desert was brutally exacting its toll. Brackett sat down on his haunches watching her, and then he took a stick and began drawing a design in the sand. For a few minutes at least, he too seemed reluctant to leave, and he sat considering Ruth, a little stupidly.

"What do ya 'spect will happen when we get to where I'm goin'?" he finally said. "You follow along where yer not wanted. What do ya 'spect will come of it?"

Ruth hated thinking about that question. "Where *are* we going, Mr. Brackett?" she asked wearily, facing him and wiping her brow. Surprisingly, he answered.

"I live about five more miles into that rocky country to the west. There's a few pinion trees there and a spring. We've built some shacks out of mud and pine. There's caves too, back in, where we go to get cool in the summer."

Ruth nodded, hoping he'd continue. He wasn't half as frightening when he spoke calmly. "My woman died a while back," he added, "without leavin' me no children. There's no one among us of marryin' age that ain't already taken or related to me."

"Where did you come from?"

Brackett scattered the sand with his stick. "My folks was part of a bunch a spirit chasers from back in Kentucky. They come out here

in the early days to find the promised land. There was some fallin' out
with the main man, I guess, an' my grandpa took his part of the family
off away from the others. By the time he died, the rest of us were pretty
well used to being on our own out here. We hunt a little, fish a little,
steal a little. Ya do what ya have to. We find our way to St. George or
Cedar ever' once in a while to trade and what not, but we don't get
along with the Mormons or anybody else, so we keep to ourselves
mostly."

Ruth edged closer to Brackett and sat opposite him on the
ground. She was far beyond any weariness she'd ever felt, and listening to him prolonged the moment when they would move on again.
But she also forced herself to be alert to anything he said. Her destiny
was wrapped up in him and his plans, as was Lucie's. "How many of
you are there?" she asked tentatively.

"Not many. Couple ol' men, my brother an' his wife, some
cousins and their kids. One woman, my father's sister, about like you
in age, maybe a little older. She ain't sassy though. Keeps her mouth
shut good and proper. She's a little teched—slow, if ya know what I
mean."

His conversational tone, in spite of his words, encouraged Ruth
to make a hoarse plea for common sense. "Mr. Brackett, why are you
doing this? It's just going to bring you trouble, and your people too.
Lucie's family will come looking for her. They won't stop until they
find her. Surely, you must know that."

"They can look all summer. It don't matter." Brackett shrugged.
"They'll never find nuthin'."

"But what about Lucie? Do you know that she's engaged to be
married? Think about that. Think of the pain you're causing. And her
young man won't just let her disappear. This desert will be scoured
from Delta to St. George, and in the end you'll be arrested with
plenty to answer for. Do you want that?"

"I want that girl; that's what I want."

"This is 1903, Mr. Brackett. The days of Indians and bandits
kidnapping women in the Wild West are over. You can't have whatever you want."

Brackett turned hard jawed again. He stood up and stared coldly at Ruth. "That's not for you to say," he growled. "Truth is, God gave this girl to me. He showed me where she was there in St. George, and He made a way for me to get her from you people. I know it was meant to be. I won't go back on what's God's doin'."

"God wouldn't *do* that," said Ruth sharply.

The man scowled at her, and then he gritted his teeth and turned away, trudging back to his horse and saddle. "Five more miles," he called over his shoulder. "You'll never make it, Sister Ruth. Yer gonna fall like a raindrop in the sand 'fore we make five miles. And it'll be for the best, ya know. My mud and pine ain't cut out for fancy ladies. No sirree."

Ruth rushed another moment with Lucie before Brackett swung into his saddle and pulled away. She reached for the girl's hand as the travois began to move. "I'm here, Lucie," she said quickly. "I won't leave you."

Lucie was awake and gripped Ruth's wrist until the horse sped up and she lost hold. "Tell Albert . . . tell Albert I'm all right." The words were barely audible, but the meaning was clear. Lucie didn't expect Ruth to keep going five more miles either.

Left standing in the dust of the travois, Ruth watched it move ahead, bumping Lucie along on its crooked sticks. Only through the grace of God was she mustering the will to follow in its tracks.

Chapter Five

MARY AGATHA

THE CLUSTER OF COOKING FIRES, pine shacks, and dugouts lay in a corner of sandstone formations hidden from casual observers by cliffs and boulders and obscured by enough trees to form a bowery and provide some protection from the sun. The camp couldn't be seen approaching from the east, but Brackett staked his horse, lifted Lucie out of the travois, and carried her over his shoulder through a small, winding slot canyon that left the world behind. Its width and height required man and animal to bend and twist and progress sideways at certain points, but it opened up on a grassy space that was adequate for the villagers and their livestock. Brackett left his horse until it could have his full attention to guide under the cliffs. Lucie was his prize now, and he carried her awkwardly through the slot, sometimes brushing against sharp rocks on either side.

***

By the time Ruth found the empty travois, she could guess Brackett's route, for the crooked slot trail was the only path. Still dazed and almost dead of thirst, she limped along the path, bracing herself on each jagged corner she encountered. At the end of the slot, a scene out of Dante spread before her: clutter and debris and animal droppings. Her hand flew to her mouth at the sight, and she groaned aloud before finally collapsing into the sparse, dry blades of prairie grass that fringed the camp. Confused and delirious, Ruth thought she was dying. But the foul smell of the camp was real. Her thirst was real. Begging for water, she suddenly felt it trickle on her lips, and she became aware of someone's hands lifting her head. A low sun was blinding her. She reached out for the arms, calling Lucie's name, and then fell back into a faint before anyone replied.

***

When Ruth awoke, she found herself lying in the mottled shade of a lean-to on a scratchy burlap rug. Slim branches woven loosely together and slanted against a sheer rock wall provided the outside cover of the shack, and through its latticed cracks she could see sunlight and hear the commotion of a village come to life. She struggled up on one elbow to squint into the shadows around her. She was light-headed, and the task of rising left her dizzy. Had her stomach not been empty, nausea would have overwhelmed her. Weakness was the culprit now, and she soon dropped back, breathing hard over the slight exertion. Where was she? And more importantly, where was Lucie?

Remembering the ugly camp scene, Ruth struggled up on her elbows to peer between the latticed branches. Clutter and filth were everywhere before her eyes: sagging tether lines for both clothes and horses; chips and kindling scattered recklessly about; smoldering, unattended fires; dead animals stretched and bloody on their drying poles; pecking chickens walking through the debris; dogs barking; and everywhere, the stench of flies, soiled food, and animal refuse. Ruth felt her stomach turn, and she dropped down again, engulfed in pure misery. As her eyes cast about the little space, she saw the Henry rifle leaning near her. The thought crossed her mind to take the gun and go, escape, lead the rescuers back to this place now that she knew where it was. But the thought was a fleeting one. She hardly had the strength to go anywhere, and she could not leave Lucie.

Where *was* Lucie? Hidden somewhere in the hollows of this stifling purgatory? Ruth felt her body quiver at the thought.

Just then, a flap covering the entrance of the lean-to was jerked aside, and Ezra Brackett filled the space. He frowned at Ruth and cursed impatiently. "Ya had to follow all the way, didn't ya? Ya had to burden us with yer needs. Ya couldn't let us be." Before Ruth could answer, he moved outside again and made room for a tall woman to duck under his arm. Ruth had never seen another like her. She looked much older than Ruth but might have been about the same age. She was mannish looking, raw and lean, with rough, leathery skin drawn tight over her high cheekbones, and long arms hanging on her bony joints. Her flat chest displayed no femininity, and her hair was combed straight back and tied into a single silver braid that hung over her left shoulder. Only her eyes seemed womanly, glowing brown and lustrous as they widened at Ruth's plight. Brackett had disappeared, and this strange figure stood in his place. Ruth reached toward her gratefully.

The woman was carrying water and a plate of food, and she knelt down to silently offer it. The tin plate was greasy and smudged with soot. On it was only a chunk of coarse bread doused in thin yellow gravy, but Ruth eagerly took the spoon. Only after the first two bites did the woman touch her wrist. "Not too fast," she ordered. "Not too much all at once."

Giving Ruth the water, the woman let her sip steadily. Then the stranger took the spoon and fed Ruth, measuring each bite. Ruth gratefully accepted, too weak to fight for the spoon or argue about it. The sopped bread was greasy and bland, but Ruth savored every mouthful and was promised more once the bowl was empty.

"Let that settle," the bony woman said. "You'll gag it up if it goes down too fast. I'll bring another plateful in a while, help ya git yer strength."

"Where's Lucie?" Ruth demanded hoarsely. "The girl who came with Brackett? Where is she? Is she all right?"

"Don't ya worry about her. She's been fed too. You her ma?"

Ruth shook her head and dropped back on the burlap. The woman gathered up the dish and canteen. "My name's Agatha," she said. "Mary Agatha." She stood up and straightened her stiff shoulders. "Ezra's my brother's boy, and I cain't always speak for what he does. All I kin do is feed the hungry and succor the weak, and I reckon I done both today." She stepped back to look judiciously at Ruth. "You've walked a long way for someone who's no kin of yours." Shrugging her knobby shoulders, she added, "Who knows what it'll get ya 'cept sore feet and a sunburn. I tol' Ez we had to feed ya. It weren't right not to, now yer here. I washed that dried blood off yer face and found some salve for your blisters. You know you got an ugly crease just behind yer ear. I put some coneflower juice on that. It musta stung a little, but it didn't wake ya up."

The woman was already ducking under the lean-to entrance before Ruth could gather words enough to answer. "Please, don't go," she breathed. "You must tell me about Lucie."

"Yer not to worry about her," said Mary Agatha. "Don't do no good to fret."

"What can you tell me about this place? Are there many women here?"

"Well, there's a few, not that it'll help ya. They's witches, most of 'em. Contrary as sows in a slaughterhouse. You'll get no smiles out of 'em, if that's what yer lookin' for."

"Then I have just you to thank for the food and water," Ruth hurried to say, hoping the woman wouldn't leave. She was a connection to Lucie and the mysteries of the camp, and Ruth reached out to her with what energy she could muster. But the odd creature had already turned her back and only paused to pull the door flap across the stream of sunshine that had briefly lighted the small enclosure.

Who was she, this Mary Agatha, strange as a homeless shadow but with food and water and a pinch of sympathy? Ruth wondered if the woman was as hard as she looked or as soft as she seemed and if the light outside meant morning or the last of a sun-glazed afternoon. Soon she realized that she had probably slept all night, for the day got brighter with the hours and her feet were cold. Someone had removed her shoes and laid them neatly together by the door. Still too weak to move, Ruth lay her head back and closed her eyes. She must have fainted, for the world went black again. When she came to her senses hours later, she knew she had not been alone. Someone had covered her with a shabby blanket, and the Henry rifle had disappeared.

Finally struggling up from the burlap mat, Ruth used the rock wall to help her keep her balance. Light-headed and unsteady, she moved slowly, stooping under the rawhide flap and into the daylight. Children scampering about paused to stare at her, and a large battered dog edged forward to nuzzle her hand. She looked around, and the scene she'd first encountered repeated itself and became vivid again. She saw a dilapidated cluster of shacks and caves circling the flat patch of ground. Animals wandered through the structures at will, leaving their droppings. A muddy, unprotected stream flowed along, its eddies sliming all they touched. The bloody carcass of a sheep was stretched across two poles near the single cooking fire, and its putrid odor drove Ruth's hand to her nose and mouth. She strangled at the smell. Dirty clothes and blankets hung by each shack or were scattered helter-skelter among the rocks. Iron pots lay about the fire, and Ruth recognized the plate she'd eaten from, overturned in the stream.

The nearest children—a boy and a girl—who'd paused to watch her were as brown as cockleburs. The boy, whose hair was a blond thatch bleached lighter by the sun, was older, about thirteen, Ruth guessed. The girl was ten, perhaps, and her tangled black hair hung down her back. They looked on silently until a feisty, foul-mouthed man appeared and yelled at them. "Go on, git!" he snapped, and the playmates were gone in a wild burst of trepidation. The man looked scornfully at Ruth but kept his distance. He was dark with cropped hair cut unevenly, and there were scars on his bristling chin and cheeks. He was slight in stature but hard muscled with a cocky, chip-on-the-shoulder posture that Ruth didn't like. She avoided eye contact and was turning away when Ezra Brackett suddenly appeared. Ruth lost no time confronting him. "Where's Lucie?" she demanded. "What have you done with her?"

Brackett shouldered past Ruth without answering. He was shirtless, wore thick suspenders pulled over the top of his faded underwear, and strode toward a dilapidated log hut shoved up against a wall of boulders some twenty yards away, pausing only when the shorter man grabbed his arm. "So this is the other woman you brung home?" said the man as they both looked sneeringly at Ruth. "Couldn't ya lose her in the desert?"

"I figured I could, but she held on." Ez Brackett looked at Ruth and shrugged.

"Why didn't ya tie her up and leave her? She'll be trouble for us now."

"I didn't have no more rope," answered Brackett, spitting to the side. "I never thought she'd follow me this far. She has an attachment to the girl, she says."

"Yes, and where is she?" Ruth insisted again, her eyes flashing. "Take me to Lucie! You've got her somewhere in this squalor, and I want to see her. Now!"

The feisty man stepped up to Ruth and shoved her with both hands. "Who are you to be makin' demands?" he cried. "Some skinny stem of a woman?"

Brackett pulled the man back. "It's all right, Cal. It don't matter. She cain't do nuthin' here. If it eases the girl's fears to see her, it might be for the best."

This did not satisfy the other man, who scowled at Ruth as Brackett motioned for her to follow him. "Since when did you go soft, Ez Brackett?" he called, still at their heels. "This is trouble fer us all. Ya know it is."

"I know who has the say 'round here," growled Brackett in the fellow's face, "and *I* say we'll let her calm the girl and help Agatha, at least fer now." He stopped and turned to Ruth. "I got ya on my hands," he said, "so you'll have to earn yer keep."

The man named Cal still complained. "You're makin' a mistake here, Ez. It's gonna bring us trouble."

"We'll use her to help with Lucie," Brackett repeated, moving once again. "At least for the time it takes to get her healed."

"At least for the healin'?" Cal barked. "Then what we gonna do with her, huh? Ya was crazy to bring her here, Ez. Once the gal is well, you tell me what we gonna do with this one."

Having heard enough, Brackett abruptly turned on the man, pushing him roughly and then tripping him as he stumbled backwards. "I don't have to tell ya nuthin'," he snarled. "When the time comes, I'll take care of things. That's all ya gotta know."

Startled, Ruth glanced back at Cal as he rolled in the dirt and finally lifted himself up, spitting in their direction. He walked away with an angry gesture, but Brackett had already turned his back. He led Ruth up a short path and into some trees where a hut sagged beneath a crude slat roof. Pushing open the door, Ruth found herself standing in a dingy room, made amber by a single lantern.

Lucie was on a small bed wedged against the stone wall, a bed which was no more than a thin mattress lifted off the floor by wood and rocks. Mary Agatha was standing near a rough plank that served as a table. But Ruth barely noticed the woman. She hurried to Lucie, and the girl squealed, her hands trembling as she reached for Ruth's arm. "Oh, Sister Fox! Oh, thank heaven! I didn't know what'd happened to you. I didn't know—"

"I'm here," said Ruth. "I'm here, Lucie!"

Lucie had obviously been fed and washed. Her color was beginning to return, though she was still frail enough to worry Ruth. She wore an oversize muslin nightgown, and her dark brown hair, completely loose, hung down around her shoulders. Her broken leg had been rewrapped in cleaner bands of cloth, and the wooden braces had been replaced with iron fire pokers bound tightly with rawhide. The bound-up leg lay stiff and straight across the bed. Lucie was indeed completely dependent on her captors, crippled as she was. But she managed a pale smile at Ruth, and even in these crude surroundings, she was beautiful. Seeing her, Ruth felt a swell of tenderness, which reinforced all her protective feelings. Somehow, someway, she would save this girl. Or she would die trying.

Dark faced, Ez Brackett stood looking on. He was sour and tense as he watched, glaring mostly at Ruth but stealing a glance or two at Lucie. He was too big for the room and uncomfortable in it, outnumbered by three women as he was, but his bulk was a reminder of the threat he posed. "You get her healed up good," he said to Mary Agatha. "A wife cain't be too lame to work." Then, with another smarmy glance at Lucie, he left, closing the door behind him and taking a dark cloud from the room.

"You're all right, Lucie? They haven't hurt you?" Ruth was full of questions once Brackett was gone, and Lucie nodded, gripping the woman's sleeve, afraid to let her go.

Mary Agatha joined Ruth at the bedside. Mary Agatha looked at Lucie with an objective eye rather than an empathetic one, but Ruth's nurturing interested her. She watched Lucie's obvious need for Ruth, her affection and trust, but the woman seemed to lack an understanding of its purpose. "I thought ya said she warn't no kin of yours," she croaked. Then she added her clinical opinion of the situation. "She'll be fine, come a month or two. Look at her eyes, alight even now." She smiled at Lucie, as she had seen Ruth do, and tweaked her cheek. "She's a pretty one, she is."

Then the woman turned and busied herself at a long shelf wedged in the chinks between the logs above the table, where dozens of jars and tin cups and bowls were scattered about. They weren't filled with food, Ruth could see, but with all sorts of natural concoctions, sticky saps, bark shavings, crushed leaves. Mary Agatha stooped over them like they were magic potions awaiting her miraculous touch. "You've got a few ugly bruises and scratches yerself," she muttered to Ruth. "I looked you over some when you was passed out in the lean-to. I got stuff here that will tackle the pain. I got stuff that will help a bone set faster. I got a black tea that will help ya sleep and settle yer stomach. I got salves to slather on yer cuts, which I already done for the girl, and poultices for every wound. That's why Ez lets me have this hut and lets that gal have it now. He knows I've got the potions that'll fix her."

"Thank you," said Ruth, "for anything you can do for us." She eyed the woman somewhat suspiciously, not yet ready to trust her completely but grateful for some kind of aid, even if it was primitive. Observing the vast assortment of saps and syrups as well as piles of crushed weeds on the shelf and table plank, Ruth was amazed. She stood gazing about, wondering how she and Lucie had ended up in this strange, repulsive place. She studied Mary Agatha, who was a mystery all by herself.

When Ruth realized that the woman was, for the moment, completely absorbed in her strange vials, she took the chance to stoop down and whisper privately to Lucie, repeating her fears. "You're sure they haven't harmed you?" she breathed. "They haven't hurt you in any way?" Lucie shook her head, and Ruth sighed audibly. "And they never will, Lucie," she murmured. "I won't let them."

"I know, Sister Fox," said Lucie softly. "Things will be all right now."

Lucie closed her eyes and seemed contented for the moment. Was it surrender? Resignation? Or Mary Agatha's potion taking its effect? Or was the girl finally somewhat at peace, knowing that Ruth was there to comfort and protect her? Ruth hoped for the latter, although she had no idea how good a guardian she could be.

Ruth saw odd Mary Agatha motioning to her, and she left the bed, still curious about both the strange woman and her apparent medicinal skills. She was a foot taller than Ruth but straight as a stick, and her shabby dress hung on her shoulders like laundry on a hook. In low tones, Mary Agatha spoke apprehensively. "I've looked close at her broke leg," she said. "When I unwrapped it, I rubbed it good with coneflower juice and juniper. That cleans the wound, ya know. But it's swollen up like a thistle cone, an' it's yeller with infection. Ez prob'ly didn't set it right neither. Too big a hurry is my guess."

"Have you got anything to treat infection?" pleaded Ruth, alarmed.

Mary Agatha turned pensively to her array of flasks and dishes. "Sometimes a good hemlock poultice draws out the flame. I tried that, but I got no promises to make. I trussed the leg up good again in hard pieces of cotton cloth, as you kin see, tying it with good tight rawhide strings and those poker rods to keep 'er stiff. We'll wait for what happens. The other leg's only deep bruised, I think. She had a few deep scratches too and a cracked rib, if I'm guessin' right, an' I done what I could for all of that."

Ruth looked back at Lucie in the bed. The girl needed a doctor, a real doctor. Ruth was used to home remedies and natural herbs, but Lucie's injury was critical. This strange woman, with all her seeds and leaves and roots, could only do so much.

"I'd hate to see that little girl lose her leg," continued Mary Agatha bluntly. "If it goes green we'll have to cut 'er off or the poor thing'll lose more than that. I done it once—cut off a leg—an' it ain't no fun. Ol' Charlie Showalter got bit by a rattler. Leg turned black as a cinder, an' we had to cut 'er off. Gave Charlie ten years more of life, but he spent it hobbled. A stump ain't no good replacement for a leg, but sometime it has to do." Mary Agatha kept talking, and as she did, her voice raised from a whisper. Ruth tried to crowd her into a corner so Lucie wouldn't wake up and hear such talk. "Yeah, I'd hate to see that little gal end up like Charlie Showalter. Ez will take her lame, I guess, but I don't feature him wantin' a wife who's missin' a leg, no matter how pretty she is otherwise."

Aghast, Ruth stiffened. She wanted to strike the woman, and she certainly wanted to quiet her. But Mary Agatha's crooked sympathy was all she and Lucie had, and Ruth held her temper and her tongue. She finally dropped into the single chair that stood next to the table plank and eyed the woman curiously. "Who are you, Mary Agatha? Are you related to Ezra Brackett or that fellow, Cal? How long have you lived like this?"

The woman pulled her chin up, startled, even offended at the question. But she liked to talk, Ruth knew, and probably never got much chance. "I'm Ezra's aunt, his pa's sister, like I tol' ya before. I'm the last of that generation. I know'd Ez since he was born, but that don't mean I care for his ways. He's grow'd up brutal, that one."

"What kind of 'family' is this? What makes this man think he can just go out and kidnap people? Just take a young girl for his wife without her consent? This girl's got a mother and father and a fiancé. They're not going to stand by and let this happen."

This drew a blank expression from the woman as if such a thing had never occurred to her. She shrugged then, twisting her thick gray braid with her fingers. "I dunno. It's been done before," she reasoned. "Ez's uncle took a wife like that once. We was in Nevada. Must be twenty years ago now. Lem come home one day with a woman we'd never seen before. She warn't as fresh as Lucie there, but she come with Lem and stayed five years or so. Then one day Lem was rooting around some rancher's barn, looking for a saddle or bridle to steal, most likely. Took a bullet to his ear from the rancher's huntin' rifle." Mary Agatha tapped her temple with a gnarled finger. "Lem's woman drifted off after that and took her two kids with her."

Ruth was unmoved by the story, stung by the squalor of this setting, repulsed by what it did to people's lives. What were she and Lucie doing here?

"No, there ain't no tellin' when some new face will appear and then move on," the craggy woman continued plaintively, turning to her flasks and bottles. "They come and go, an' it's no concern of mine. That is, if they ain't sick or bleedin'. If they are, they find ol' Agatha, an' I do what I kin less they're too far gone for anyone to care."

Ruth still couldn't believe what she was hearing. She glanced at Lucie, wondering how she had handled letting this woman salve her wounds and wrap her leg. Mary Agatha was a crone, out of some ancient fairy tale. "Are you married?" Ruth questioned. "Do you have children? Do you have a husband who keeps you here?"

Mary Agatha's grin showed several missing teeth, but her eyes flashed merrily. "Take another look at me, Sister Ruth, and answer yer own question!" she laughed. "No, I got no kids and no man. No one's ever took a second glance at me. But I don't mind. I tend to the folks that's here. Nourish the hungry and succor the weak, that's what I do. I took an interest in saps and ointments and the healin' power of flowers when I was just a girl. Folks begun to come to me when they was hurt or ailin' even then. I figure that's what God wants of me . . . to tend to folks. I ain't much to look at, but I got a gift that keeps folks comin' 'round from time to time."

These words softened Ruth a little. She glanced again at Lucie, who was drowsing, and felt some appreciation for what this woman had done. The broken leg looked well bound, and Lucie's pain had eased enough to let her sleep. Ruth eyed the array of tin plates and jars on Mary Agatha's shelf. "What is all this? You've got a laboratory here."

"Like I tol' ya, it's my potions, ever'thing from prickly pear poultice to juniper tea. I got a couple things that ain't even from these parts. Sometimes we light on a trader or a drummer that has seeds and crushed up leaves from up north or even from the East. They keep crushed leaves in their pokes to roll smokes with if they got no tobacco. An' I trade it off of 'em sometimes. Ezra lets me keep what I gather here in the cabin cuz it's the only real house we got. Only real bed as well." She nodded toward Lucie breathing heavily now and sound asleep. "It sets up a smell in here sometimes," she conceded, "but I don't mind. It keeps the others and all their foolishness away."

Remembering the smell of rot outside, Ruth doubted anything was worse, but she let Mary Agatha go on talking. This was where she and Lucie found themselves, and Ruth knew she needed to assess the situation and act judiciously for Lucie's sake. The herbs and remedies spread before her were of the most primitive kind, and she doubted whether they had ever really healed anyone. But they were all that Lucie had. The "cabin" was crooked on its foundation, a hut of logs, stones, and boards chinked together during some previous time. From the outside it looked like it might tumble down at the slightest nudge, but inside it was sturdy. There was a thick roof of slat boards but no windows and no fireplace. With the bed and table, there was hardly room enough to turn around. The floor was warped; the dust was thick. But the cabin offered shelter, and it was all the captives had—a shabby hut and this strange woman, who stirred about in her herb and sap collection like it was a king's treasure.

"Tell me about Ezra's wife," pressed Ruth, almost afraid to ask. "How did she die?"

"Oh, that was Elsie. Elsie Wales. She was always sick, poor thing. Skinny and pale as Dolly's ghost. She never could give Ez no babies, and she finally got the hack last winter and coughed herself to death. I tried to help her with St. John's wort and peppermint, but she was too weak to even swallow after a while. She's buried over in the next draw, where there's a little bit of soft ground. I done the best I could for her. I even told Ez to ride somewhere and find a doctor when she got so bad. He wouldn't do it. I think he plum gave up on Elsie when she couldn't have no babies or do any heavy work."

"And that's what he wants for Lucie," murmured Ruth soberly.

"I ain't sayin' I agree with the way Ez goes about things," Mary Agatha asserted quickly, "but for us desert folks there's sometimes no other way. Ez believes God directs his path, even if it leads him off a cliff. He learned that from his grandpa, and it's an idea that's rooted deep inside him like some kind of demon seed. We've learned to live with Ezra's convictions. He won't have it no other way."

"How many of you are there? I saw two children outside, and that Cal fellow . . ."

"Cal is Ez's brother and as contrary as a banty rooster. His wife is Clara Tophorn, whose folks used to preach to us—till they both up and died. Them two kids you saw were most likely Luke and Tilda.

One of 'em belongs to Jacob Royal and his woman. The girl, Tilda, is half Indian. One of Clara's sisters run away once and brought baby Tilda home when she come slinkin' back a year later. Cal and Clara have a couple of younger ones. Another family, the Grovers, is part of us, only Joe Grover never says that much. He leaves the arguing to Ez and Cal, who do it plenty enough. Jacob Royal sticks his nose in time to time, but it's mostly Ez who has the say in what we do."

"So the others just let him go out and steal and kidnap and commit crimes? Don't they know it will bring trouble to *all* of them in the end?"

"We've lived like this a long time," shrugged Mary Agatha, toying with a measuring spoon. "It's all we know."

"You've never thought of leaving?"

"Where would I go?"

"Surely, you can't think this will last," said Ruth, mystified. "Surely, you know Lucie's family and mine will search until they find us. You can't go on living like this, stealing, kidnapping, treating women like—"

"Twenty-five years," interrupted Mary Agatha. "Twenty-five years since my brother Elmer first brought us out here, an' nobody's found us yet. We're like ghosts, Sister Ruth. We kin fade into the air whenever trouble comes." She waved her hands in Ruth's face, letting her fingers dance. "We slip away like magic, yes sirree." She laughed then, a teasing, cackling chortle, and Ruth was happy to let her turn back to her strange and sticky potions. When Ruth again used those salves on her own wounds and bruises, she found them surprisingly soothing in spite of their questionable origin. Perhaps Mary Agatha knew magic after all.

Chapter Six
ENEMIES AND ALLIES

RUTH MOVED A BURLAP MAT into the hut and did her best to sleep on the hard floor next to Lucie's bed. Mary Agatha found another ragged quilt for her, which offered some cover but little comfort. The herb remedies Mary Agatha conjured up seemed to take the edge off Lucie's pain and help her sleep, but Ruth was anxious to be close whenever the girl woke up with a start and remembered where she was.

Mary Agatha brought more of the coarse bread and broth that afternoon and thick mush the following morning, though neither Lucie nor Ruth could eat more than a few bites. The two women lifted the girl and helped her use a chamber pot. It was awkward, embarrassing, and painful for Lucie, and Ruth vowed to find a more efficient and comfortable way to see to the girl's personal needs once her leg could take some weight. But in the meantime, Ruth was grateful that Mary Agatha was there to help her. It was what they had.

Lucie neither whined nor objected to any of the circumstances as long as Ruth was there, but Ruth found the girl still fragile in so many ways. "When you were gone," Lucie had whispered more than once, "when I didn't know where you were, I couldn't breathe, I was so afraid. I thought I was dying." She would clutch Ruth's hand. "My mother will be grateful you were here."

"Don't speak of dying, Lucie." Ruth constantly tried to sap the power of her faith. "The Lord has not forgotten us. You're going to be all right."

But she knew a brutal threat remained.

The first evening after Mary Agatha had gone, Brackett came again and looked ponderously at Lucie while Ruth watched his every move. She was getting to know the man, becoming familiar with his body language and his gestures, and she tried to be optimistic. He had been smarmy and repulsive, but he *had* lifted the wagon to save Lucie, and he hadn't hurt Ruth. He could have tied her up and left her in the heat as Cal had suggested. He could have killed her. He didn't seem to care about Tom Leavitt's death, which he had caused, but Ruth nursed some hope for a moment that the man was not entirely a monster. Then he again made clear his intentions, and she shuddered in her soul.

"She's got her color back," he muttered that first night, hovering over Lucie. He stood stiff and tall and awkward in the cabin, taking up most of the cramped space. "Might be six weeks for that leg to heal so's she can be up and around," he judged and then added sharply, "I don't want to wait that long to take her to wife."

Ruth swallowed hard.

Brackett continued to leer at Lucie, who refused to look at him. "Yep, you people sure shoulda let me have her when I first stopped ya on the trail. Coulda saved a whole lotta trouble for ever'body."

Ruth remained quiet, but her dark eyes drilled through him, scorning his evil with all her soul. He was bullish and strong and in control, but she was determined, like David, to somehow master the giant. She followed him when he left, and on the doorstep, hopefully out of Lucie's hearing, she confronted him again. "Surely you have some feeling, Mr. Brackett. You won't bother Lucie while she's crippled. Only an animal would act like that."

"Well, what makes you think I ain't a wolf or bear?" Brackett thundered, lunging toward her with mock viciousness. He chortled as Ruth backed away, startled at the gesture. But Brackett had just begun to growl, and his tone turned serious. "Ya think 'cause I fixed up this girl's leg and give her a bed to sleep in that I've gone soft?" he seethed. "Ya think 'cause I didn't leave you tied up to a cedar tree that I've turned clammy? Why, Sister Ruth, you been readin' your Bible too long. I got no weak feelings. I fixed up Lucie for just one reason. God gave her to me for a wife, and I aim to have a woman that kin walk! As for you, Cal was right. I shoulda left ya where I found ya fer the buzzards ta eat."

He stomped away then without looking back, and Ruth was left to stare through the darkness at him until he disappeared. Brackett's sudden rage frightened her and smothered any hope she had that he could be reasonable. It was clear that Lucie's injuries would only keep him away so long and that Ruth by herself was no match for his temper. Trembling, she turned back into the hut and did the best she could to busy herself about the room until the shock of Brackett's words wore off. When she finally bent toward Lucie, there were tears in the girl's eyes. She had heard too much.

"Try not to listen to that man's cursed tongue, dear Lucie," Ruth pleaded, dropping to the bedside. "It's an evil man's bravado. Help will come before Ez Brackett can hurt you."

Lucie squeezed Ruth's hand but remained silent for a moment. The girl closed her eyes and frowned, consumed by misery. Her voice lost all its music when she spoke.

"Life's been too good to me," she murmured. "I've been pampered into shallowness, Sister Fox. A week ago, all I ever had to think about was singing and dancing, wearing pretty clothes, and planning fancy parties. My wedding was to be the social highlight of our neighborhood. It's all I had to worry about. Now look where I am. I never thought the world could be as grim as this. The way these people live . . . I can't believe it. But they haven't had the privileges I've had—the gospel, an education, loving parents. All they know is cruelty and squalor . . . maybe God is trying to humble me or punish me for my self-centered ways."

"Don't blame yourself for any of this," Ruth answered gently but with affirmation in her voice. "God had nothing to do with Ezra Brackett's actions, and poverty gives no one the right to behave like an animal." She paused to take the girl's hand and hold it in her own, adding stoutly, "We'll get through this, Lucie, you and I, and it will be those very things you spoke of that will help us—the gospel, the love of others, and even the beauty we strive to be a part of in this world. Those things give us the strength to carry on."

She coaxed a wan smile out of Lucie and hoped her words would make a difference.

***

The next morning Mary Agatha unwrapped Lucie's leg to inspect her work. The wound was ugly, but the woman seemed pleased. "Look at that," she said to Ruth. "The swellin's gone down, and the edges of the tear are knittin' fine already. We got a fast healer here."

Ruth, peering intently over the woman's shoulder, shot a glance at Lucie's pale face on the pillow, thankful that she couldn't see how terrible things were. "It's still badly inflamed," she whispered, startled again by the tattered gash that had exposed the bone.

"'Course it's flamin'," snapped Mary Agatha. "It's as red as raw liver in a butcher shop. But it ain't green, so that's a good sign. My coneflower juice is workin' its miracles. I'll slather some more of it on her and wrap things up tight again." Then she bent to speak to Lucie with her rustic candor. "I know what yer feelin'. The pain is gonna swell from time to time. Wounds gone cold can throb and smolder even while they're healin'. I'll keep ya soused with my black root tea, but ya got a ways to go before the deep down ache lets up, most likely."

Lucie gritted her teeth and clenched the bedcover with her fists, saying nothing. She watched as Ruth and Mary Agatha wrapped the leg again, leaving it stiff and heavy in its iron frame, but Lucie kept her head against the pillow and refused to look at her injury. Ruth knew it was more than throbbing pain that subdued Lucie, more than a wound gone cold.

After Mary Agatha trundled off, Ruth tried to offer comfort. She knew that Lucie was absorbing a grim reality. She had much more to fear than the pain and trauma of a broken leg or being trapped under a wagon. Ruth began to see surrender or resignation in the girl again, and she tried to fight against it with all the strength she could muster.

"Look, Lucie. Look what I have." Ruth smiled as the idea suddenly dawned on her. Slowly, she took from her pocket the silver case she'd saved, the one with Albert's picture and the little calendar marked in red. "I found this before we left the wreckage. You know what it is and what it means." She slipped the case into Lucie's hand and watched a glimmer return to her eyes as she opened it.

"Oh, poor Bertie," Lucie whispered. "I wonder if I'll ever see him smile like this again."

"Of course you will." Ruth stroked the girl's hair. The amber glow in the room lent a sepia tone to Lucie's cheeks, as if she were peering out from some faraway place. Ruth struggled to bring her back. "Mark the calendar, dear girl," she pleaded. "Count the days. Help can't be far away."

The opened case trembled in Lucie's fingers for a moment. "I'll use the black end of the pencil," she finally murmured, "until we're free."

***

Mary Agatha came with broth at dinnertime, and before the end of the day, two other women of the camp made an appearance at the hut, Clara Brackett and Jacob Royal's wife, a short, pear-shaped, middle-aged woman called Gertie. Clara's last name was actually Tophorn, Ruth had been told, but she was Cal Brackett's wife—by common law at least. Gertie Royal never left her side. They were both hard, disheveled, rough-hewn women who took little interest in Mary Agatha's medicinal concoctions but hovered over Lucie with the curiosity of long-haired demons waiting to pounce.

Behind them, the boy, Luke Royal, peered around his mother's skirt. He was standing on one bare foot, scratching the back of his leg with the other grimy toe. His eyes were wide and brown, and his hair was shaggy. They all seemed piqued and full of resentment. Lucie was another mouth to feed, and a useless one at that, since she was injured and in no shape to work. They also regarded Ruth with dubious glances. This woman was not one of them. She would undoubtedly cause trouble.

"Leave it to Ez Brackett to find himself a scratchy, cackling hen and bring it home to roost," complained Clara when she thought Ruth couldn't hear. Her pale, watery eyes sunk low in their deep sockets, and there was no kindness in them. "So ya busted yer leg, huh, girl?" She turned to Lucie. "That'll keep ya from the hoe and shovel for a month a Sundays."

"Yeah, she'll miss a dance or two," chirped Gertie Royal, "an' I'll bet she likes to dance, as pretty as she is." She took hold of Lucie's arm, and as Ruth jumped forward, Lucie herself jerked her arm away.

"Please don't touch me," Lucie said with spite.

"A snippy one too." The woman scowled and then turned her attention and her pale eyes to Ruth. "Well, I'll tell ya who ya want to stay clear of, and that's ol' Agatha there. Ol' Mary Agatha, the poison-potion maker. Ain't that right, Clara? I wouldn't let that witch touch me with that sap o' hers. She'll kill ya if she can and blame the roots and flowers. No, I wouldn't let her touch nuthin' you hold dear."

"You let me touch ya quick enough last winter when ya had the whooping cough," spit Mary Agatha defiantly. "Yer boy too, as I recall." Mary had spooned the leftover broth into a pewter flask for some mysterious brew. "If I'd meant to poison ya, ya wouldn't be around to squawk about it now!"

Gertie ignored the words and shrugged as she turned again to Ruth. "If yer this girl's ma, ya might want to have a palaver with her. She don't look ready to be a wife yet, or to cotton to our ways."

"Too much dancin'," added Clara smugly, "an' not enough workin'."

"Go on, git, you two!" Mary Agatha suddenly shrieked. "Go on. Git outa here. We got no room fer ya, ya nosey witches."

She scattered Clara and Gertie, and they backed quickly out the door, still cackling to themselves. Mary Agatha looked after them until they had disappeared down the path, the dirty boy trailing along, and then she turned to Ruth and Lucie. "Brainless as turnip roots, those two." She leaned over her table again with its array of medicinal jars and mortars. "Poison, hah! As if I'd waste my potions on the likes of them."

For the moment, Ruth was glad to have Mary Agatha on her side.

***

That night around the central cooking fire, arguments began again about the danger Brackett had inflicted on the camp by bringing the women there. While their wives said nothing, hovering on the outskirts of the circle, Grover and another man seemed to side with foul-mouthed Cal, while he raged at Ezra Brackett. Not everyone had Cal's vinegar, but most agreed that this new circumstance meant trouble. Jacob Royal, a slight man who had brought a Bible to the circle, opined quietly that Brackett's desire for a pretty wife might have outweighed his common sense. Even nascent support emboldened Cal, and his anger grew as the night wore on. "These women ain't wanderers or runaways," he cried. "These are fancy, house-bred women. Their people will come looking for 'em, and they won't give up easy!"

Hearing the voices, Ruth crept from the hut, leaving Mary Agatha with Lucie. She found the lean-to where she had spent her first night in the camp. It was closer to the fire pits, and from behind its latticed branches she could listen to the men and watch their faces. "We got a cow here that belongs to that farmer over by Cedar," Cal continued. "It's got his brand. We got gear and equipment we took off saddle tramps and wranglers, all kinds of stuff. We cain't have the law nosin' around here, Ez, and they'll be here, sure as anything, once they find that wrecked transit wagon. They ain't gonna give up them women, no matter how much wind and sand they have to cut through to find 'em."

Ruth wondered if Brackett had told his companions about Tom Leavitt's death, another reason the law would certainly be "nosin' around."

"I thought you had your eye on some Indian girl," Grover said timidly to Brackett, and then Cal took up the cause again. Ruth listened to the wild-eyed Cal and was put off by his temper. He was impulsive, too quick to boil over instead of steep. That fellow Grover and Jacob Royal seemed more pliable. More sympathetic, perhaps? She wondered but then decided they were passive men, screwed down by an overpowering sense of their own insignificance. They wouldn't stand up to Brackett; they were too afraid of him.

Brackett's argument was clear. "God directed me to Lucie Cole," he declared to everyone in the circle. "I know that for a fact. I know'd it when I first seen her in that mercantile store in St. George. She was at the counter buying cloth and such and speakin' to the clerk, and there was music in her voice. I heard it. A feelin' come over me, and I knew it was God tellin' me about this girl."

"But how can ya be so sure, Ez, with just one glance like that?" asked Royal. "She don't seem our kind."

Brackett was quick to counter him. "She ain't our kind. She's one of them holy Mormons, an' don't ya think it pleasures me to filch one of theirs? I'll say it does. But I was careful not to move too quick. I tracked that gal for days, followed her on the streets and at school. I even went to Sunday meetin' a time or two. I seen her with her friends. Once I seen her playin' a ball game with 'em in a meadow. I could tell that she was young and strong and had some grit in 'er. The more I watched, the more I know'd she was the one. God confirmed it, and I ain't goin' back on it now."

"What about the woman?" cried Cal again. "What we gonna do with her?"

"I ain't decided. She cain't do us no harm an' she cain't walk outa here, so I'm bidin' my time with it. If her people come like ya say, maybe we could make a trade. But I don't see 'em findin' us. We've vanished into these mountains before. We'll do it again if it comes to that."

Jacob Royal fingered the Bible on his lap. "If God gave you that girl, Ez, don't ya think ya need someone to say some words . . . to make it a marriage that's blessed and right with heaven?"

"Words is words," declared Brackett impatiently. "I walked through the sun and slept under the stars at night to get this girl. Heaven looked down on me. Words is nuthin' next to that. You can rattle off some scripture if you want, but I figure heaven's part's all been taken care of."

"How long ya gonna wait?" asked Royal, still concerned with propriety.

"Well, I ain't gonna wait too long, I'll tell ya that!" Ez was boisterous. "The girl's all pale and cloudy from her pain. As limp and gray as a wet pup. I'd like to see her perk up a bit. I wanna see a little life in her 'fore the weddin'." The men laughed, and Brackett warmed to his audience. "But keep yer Bible handy, Royal, cuz I ain't waitin' too long, no sirree."

"Come on, Ez," cried one of the men. "I say you can't wait ten days for that little gal, young and pretty as she is."

"Ten days," shouted Cal, liking the odds, "busted leg or not!"

"All right! Ten days it is," bellowed Ez, "and I've got a silver dollar says I can do it. Put yer own up beside mine. You kin all draw a day, and I swear I'll outlast 'em all. One of us'll be rich come time for the weddin'."

Even feisty Cal had a dollar to wager, and with the others, he goaded Ezra into chipping an *X* into a board to mark the promise. "We'll nail it here," he said, leaning the board against a cider barrel, "and we'll make a scratch on 'er ever'day until there's nine of 'em and the *X* comes up. We'll give the loot to Jake Royal to keep with his Bible. If Ez lasts the ten days, he gets the money. If he don't," Cal howled, "the fella who's day it is when Jake opens up the book to say the words, well, that fella gets the pile."

All of the men put up what they could—grimy coins and trinkets. Grover offered his pocket watch. Cal passed it all to Jacob Royal. "Here, Jake," he said, "keep it all wrapped up with your scriptures. Then we know it's safe."

"Ya think you've got me, don't ya?" Ezra roared playfully at his brother. "But I ain't no fool. Whatever happens, I'm a winner here. Ya know that, don't ya?"

"Then it won't hurt to let us have a little fun." Cal jammed his knife into the empty cider barrel and grinned. The plan was fixed, and soon Ruth heard raucous laughter coming from the circle. What had begun as an argument over Ezra's endangering the camp had turned into a cruel game played by ignorant men.

Ruth was repulsed by all of it. That these men would gamble over Lucie turned her stomach. But the ten-day pledge gave her a glimmer of hope as well. By her calculation it had already been five days since Fenton Meade had made it to Modena. Surely rescue would arrive well before another ten. Why, it would probably come tomorrow! Certainly before the week was out.

But a dark shadow crossed her mind. Ezra Brackett was governed more by his base instincts than his need for a few coins and trinkets. The pledge would provide nothing but a hesitation if Brackett grew impatient. Suddenly it struck Ruth that in the very lean-to where she crouched, the Henry rifle had once been, and loaded or not she needed it. It was gone now or at least moved. Had it really disappeared, or had it only been shoved aside?

She looked about in the shadows, feeling with her hands along the ground. She was certain the rifle had been there two days ago when she'd first come to her senses. In her mind, she could still see it, leaning there, with perhaps a single bullet in the pipe. But after covering every inch and every corner of the space, she wondered if it had all been her imagination. Bullet or no bullet, the Henry .44 was gone, and Ruth went back to the cabin empty-handed, her heart pounding over what lay ahead.

Ruth's protective feelings became an obsession. Mary Agatha and her potions might heal Lucie's wounds, but Ruth was there to salve her soul. She made no mention of Ez Brackett's wager to either Lucie or Mary Agatha, but each morning she grimly watched Jacob Royal scratching a mark on the board nailed to the cider barrel.

Slash by slash, three days went by. Brackett stayed away, perhaps making an effort to avoid temptation, but Ruth was ever wary and kept the chair jammed against the cabin door at night.

She thought of turning to Mary Agatha for help in finding the rifle or even in escaping on one of the horses tethered to a line at the edge of the camp. But could she trust the stranger? Ruth had no idea where Mary Agatha slept and didn't ask. The woman simply appeared every morning, completed her tasks, and talked incessantly. She always brought clean water and food, such as it was, and showed Ruth a place nearby where she'd fashioned her own little fire pit. Most of the camp's cooking was done communal style over the center fires, but some of the women kept individual pits as well. There, they baked bread in makeshift stone ovens and dried the fruit and vegetables they stole or gathered wild. Sometimes there were shriveled onions, turnips, carrots, and berries. The center pits were reserved for wild meat—animals the men killed for the entire camp. Gertie Royal made a thick mush from ground wheat every morning, and a single cow provided milk to wash it down. Most of the food was repulsive, and Ruth ate sparingly.

Two more slashes marked the board before she realized that she was becoming ill from sleepless nights and poor nutrition, and she made an effort for Lucie's sake to eat whatever was offered and more regularly—and to see that Lucie did the same.

Each morning, Mary Agatha dutifully brought mush to the cabin for Ruth and Lucie, and she sweetened it from her secret stash of molasses or wild honey, which she produced proudly, telling Ruth she "hid up" such treasures from the other women for mocking her. She had some sugar too, acquired from a traveler she encountered on the Modena road. "Traded him a poke of chicory to ease his stomach growl," she explained. "He toted a little sugar for coffee on the trail, but he said he'd take it bitter if the chicory would cure his gripe. I promised him it would."

"What about Ez Brackett's coffee?" Ruth mused, still puzzling over the man. "I suppose he takes it bitter too." Mary Agatha looked at her quizzically, and Ruth was obliged to add, "There's little sweetness in him."

Mary Agatha was proud of her innovations, such as the way she'd purified the camp's drinking water by pouring it through a clean stretch of woven burlap. "It strains out most of the dirt and bugs," she told Ruth. Ruth was grateful to learn that the drinking and cooking water came from a natural spring above the camp. The dirty grit flowing in the stream that skirted the fire pits was more than she could stand.

On the other hand, Mary seemed unconcerned with the filth outside. Her obsessive pleasure was in her natural medicine concoctions—potent teas from thistles and sunflowers and the bark of mountain ash, poultices from prickly pears, and hemlock to relieve the pain of open wounds and lacerations. "Look here," she showed Ruth proudly. "A while back I got me some fennel leaves, those threadlike ones that smell so strong. Over here is butterfly weed. Its tea can help yer stomach if you keep it weak. It might kill ya if ya don't. Then there's the catnip here in the blue box that an herb trader give me once when

I was in Modena. Steep that up an' it'll sweat a cold right out of ya and then put ya sound to sleep. I swear it will!" Mary Agatha puttered with the various cups and bottles. "Yep, two strong gulps of the fennel tea 'll kill ya or light yer gut on fire. Add a little of this or that, and you'll sleep for hours—if yer lucky—and wake up rarin' to empty yer belly of anything it's got. Either way, yer gonna be down a spell, sicker than a hound dog in a snake pit. But if it don't kill ya, it'll heal ya," she concluded, "like a lot of things in this ol' world."

"Lucie needs a real doctor," Ruth urged one day. "You know she does. Your herbs are fine, Mary, but we can't let Lucie lose her leg."

"It's happened before," the woman shrugged. "It'll serve Ez right if he finds he's got a lame one on his hands."

This kind of graceless talk repulsed Ruth, but she was coming to understand the kind of woman she was dealing with. Mary Agatha seemed to be a strange medieval leaf gatherer, a spirit from another time or planet, and Ruth began to feel affection for her as she found herself dependent on any wisdom the woman might put forth. Given their surroundings and the lack of education and refinement of these people, it was only natural that a raw, unvarnished attitude would prevail in this forsaken place. It showed itself from time to time on Mary Agatha's lips.

Often Ruth watched the children—Luke and Tilda and the others—sneak around, sometimes playing tricks and teasing the odd woman. They laughed at Mary Agatha behind her back. "Skinny Agatha," they sniped, and Ruth heard them say far worse. The entire village viewed the woman with disdain, as if she were some kind of witch or sorcerer. Clara Tophorn, Gertie Royal, and the other women generally ignored her, chattering only among themselves. The men were loath to give any credit whatsoever to her skills, although they were willing enough to accept her service when it was required. Slowly, Ruth's own dependence on Mary Agatha grew stronger too. There were five scratches on the cider barrel, and Lucie desperately needed any ally she could get.

Ruth broached the subject early one morning when Mary Agatha arrived unexpectedly just as the sun was rising. The early knock at the door had frightened Ruth, awakening her from a troubled dream.

Opening it, she scanned the sleeping camp, alert for trouble, but the woman elbowed past her, anxious to do some boilin' before breakfast. "Boilin'" meant heating one of her mixtures on a tin holder which stood on a three-legged brace above a candle. It was better for small items than a campfire was and could be handled on the table close to the precious medicinal shelf.

As Mary set to work, the hut grew quiet again except for the clink of her spoon and the occasional creaking of the chair. Ruth glanced at Lucie, still drowsing, and then asked pointedly, "Where does Mr. Brackett spend the nights?"

Mary Agatha had already set a tin cup on a tripod brace above the candle. She was ready to heat the water and experiment with her pastes and potions. Ruth's question about Brackett gave her pause, and then she answered with a wry smile. Suddenly rising from her work and setting the cup aside, she took Ruth's arm and moved back to the door, opening it only wide enough for both of them to barely peek past the frame.

"There's a cave over there where Ez sleeps," the woman whispered, "a cave in the rocks back past the trees. But ya kin always tell when he's got up."

"How?"

Mary Agatha pointed a bony finger toward the center fire pit some twenty-five yards away. "Ya see that tree limb there stuck in the ground for a post? That one next to the kindlin' pile? There's two twigs stickin' out like hooks off either side. One's lower than the other. Ya see what I'm talkin' about?"

Ruth nodded. The thick branch was straight and sturdy, about five feet tall.

"There's a big coffee mug hangin' on that high twig. D' ya see it? That cup belongs to Ez, an' the first thing he does ever' morning, rain or shine, is take that cup from the twig an' have his coffee. Rain or shine. Sometimes before his shirt is buttoned. He comes and pours his coffee ever'day, drinkin' it first thing. Sets an hour doin' it too. Then he puts the mug back on the low twig till evenin'. That means Gertie needs to rinse it out. Then she puts it back on the high twig, an' it better be there when Ez reaches for it, or there's the devil to pay.

That's just how it is." Mary Agatha looked at Ruth and smiled, proud of her wisdom in the matter. "So, ya kin always tell if Ez has rose up yet. If it's mornin' and the cup is hangin' there on the high twig, he's still snorin' in his cave like a big ol' grizzly bear."

"I'll keep that in mind," said Ruth dryly, eyeing the pewter cup and wondering where Brackett had stolen it.

Mary Agatha continued to intrigue Ruth. *You crippled mortal soul,* Ruth wanted to cry out to the woman. *You've got more wit and natural skill than anybody here. Why do you let these people tell you how to live? Why are you content to let this band of thieves rule over you?* But Ruth spoke only in her thoughts, looking on in wonder as Mary Agatha busied herself at her medicinal shelf. Ruth was sure that such rebellious ideas had never occurred to her.

After telling Ruth about the coffee mug, Mary had turned back to her work, losing herself with great intensity in the pods of a desert willow. There was a strange prescience in the woman. Ruth watched as the morning deepened and the camp began to stir, and just as Mary Agatha predicted, Ezra Brackett, still yawning and dragging his suspenders, found his coffee cup on the high twig and demanded the boiling pot from Tessie Grover, who was fixing breakfast. Yes, Ruth was coming to understand that Mary Agatha, with her powers of observation and medicinal knowledge, had more natural skill than anyone in the camp.

Chapter Seven
MIDNIGHT OIL

Watching the notches on the cider barrel board grow to six, Ruth worried restlessly about Brackett's intentions. With no sign of a rescue team, her anxieties grew raw and painful, and she could hardly bear to think of what poor Lucie was feeling. Again, she considered telling Mary Agatha about the wager and why they needed to find the rifle and defend Lucie at all cost, but Mary seemed oblivious to the gravity here. "I reckon we'll be havin' a weddin' once the young gal's on her feet," the woman sometimes chortled to herself.

Before his wager at the campfire, Brackett had come each night to hover over Lucie. Early on, when she was still weak and feverish, he did nothing more than that, pondering the situation with impatience and taking a foul mood with him when he left. Mary Agatha accepted this without discussion. But Ruth was always tense, anxious. The slightest sound of the creaky cabin door would leave her tense. Brackett's raucous voice, laughing, yelling to his camp mates, or growling at the horses kept her on edge. She found a narrow slit in the chinks of the cabin wall where she could watch unseen the stirrings of the camp, and there she kept an eye out for anyone approaching, especially Brackett, whom she feared. But she kept her frightened thoughts from Mary Agatha, whom she did not yet fully trust.

The coffee mug on the twig became Ruth's first focus every morning. Brackett headed for the cup the moment he appeared each day, often before he was fully dressed. Once, Ruth saw the boy, Luke Royal, skitter slyly up to the twig and take the mug. The boy mischievously hid the mug behind his back and edged away, obviously bent on playing a joke. But the owner of the cup was in no joking mood when he came yawning and stretching toward the fire pit some moments later.

"You little devil!" he roared at Luke. "Ya touch my cup again, I'll box yer ear!" With that, he cuffed the youngster soundly on his ear and sent him screaming to his mother.

Yes, Ruth feared Ezra Brackett. The ugly profanities he uttered around the camp repulsed her, but they signaled where he was at any given moment and what was drawing his attention, and Ruth was always alert for any change. Once, as she kept watch through the slit between the logs, she saw Brackett pause at the bottom of the path and glower in the direction of the hut, his eyes riveted on it, his chin determined. He made a motion to approach, and Ruth's heart froze. When he changed his mind and turned away, it was still several moments before she could breathe again. She thanked God for the ugly wager. A few grimy coins and trinkets seemed to be all that was keeping Brackett away from Lucie at the moment. But how long could his stubborn desire for the money last? How long would his pride keep him from what he really wanted? These were terror-filled days for Ruth, who prayed for strength with all the faith she had.

And through the week, as the slashes on the cider barrel board increased, there was one hope Ruth clung to. Just hours after Brackett's campfire wager was set, Mary Agatha provided the new connection that bolstered Ruth's faith. It was a simple thing, but as the slashes on the board marked the anxious days, an extraordinary bond developed between the women. It was forged at night while the camp was quiet and even Lucie was asleep. It came from an unexpected source, and while it didn't completely allay Ruth's suspicions about Mary Agatha's loyalty, it gave her a tenuous thread into the woman's heart.

"Yer an educated lady, ain't ya?" Mary had asked. "Ya been to school?"

"Yes," Ruth nodded. She was sitting on her burlap bed listening to Lucie breathe fitfully in her sleep. Brackett's wager was fresh in her mind, and she paid Mary little attention at first. It was late, and for some reason the woman had lingered over her saps and seeds instead of leaving as she usually did.

"Kin ya read?" she pressed.

"Yes, of course." Ruth looked up. "I write too. Poems and speeches mostly. I love words as you love your wildflowers, Mary Agatha. Words can be healing, just as your ointments are."

"What kind of books you got to read?" Mary Agatha seemed entranced.

"Well, I'm a church woman. That's why Lucie calls me Sister Ruth or Sister Fox. So I read the scriptures—the Bible, which you probably know, and other books that we Mormons have. I'm fond of all great books, Shakespeare, the poets, the great writers of our time and the past. There's no end to wonderful things to read."

The woman considered this but said no more about it. Soon she pushed her work aside and silently disappeared into the night as she always had. It was only much later, after Ruth was asleep and the entire camp was quiet and the candlewick had flickered out, that the door creaked and Mary Agatha peeked around its edge. She was stealthy, like a ghost, pushing at the chair that barred her path only enough to awaken Ruth, who rose to let her in. "Mary, what is it?" A wave of panic rolled through her heart. "Is something wrong?"

Mary Agatha seemed secretive and didn't answer. While Ruth closed the door and replaced the chair, Mary lit a fresh candle, placed it in the lantern, and motioned for Ruth to return to her bed on the floor. Then, bringing the lantern there, Mary Agatha fell to her knees. "Sister Ruth," she whispered. "Look here at what I got."

Ruth was surprised to find Mary Agatha holding a shabby Bible in one hand, and, shockingly, a Book of Mormon in the other. "Look what I got," she repeated. "Ol' Jacob Royal thinks he has the only Bible here, but I got this one hidden away in my mama's stuff." She lifted the Book of Mormon in her other hand and looked at it. "And this here is you Mormons' holy book. I know it is. Someone brought it to us years ago. Grandpa Brackett threw it away, but I didn't have no books, so I saved it. I kept it in my treasures where no one knows I got it."

Ruth was astonished. She took the Book of Mormon from Mary Agatha's hand, if only to assure herself that it was real. "Have you read this?" she asked.

Mary Agatha seemed surprised then ashamed as she took the book into her hands again, patting it gently. "I'd like to say I have. But I don't know how . . . to read, that is. I never learned."

Ruth's mouth dropped open. She looked at Mary Agatha with sudden tenderness and fresh respect. "Why . . . why have you kept these books if you can't read them?" she asked incredulously.

"I've tried to read 'em," said Mary Agatha hopefully. "I've turned the pages and tried to figure out the words. Sometimes Clara teaches the kids some of the letters, and I listen in, an' after they shoo me away I take what I remember and try to pick words out of this book, but I don't think Clara knows as much as she thinks she does."

"I'll teach you, Mary Agatha," said Ruth quickly. "I'll teach you all the letters and their sounds. I'll teach you to read this book!"

"You could do that?"

"Why, of course I could. Why, there are lines in both these books that you don't even have to read more than once. You can learn them by heart as I have. They become part of you."

"Well, I know'd some of the stories. Grandma Brackett was big on stories from the Bible when we was kids, ya know. The shepherd boy, David, with his sling, was one we liked. How he killed the giant with a little stone. And that fella Daniel in the lion's den, and how the king felt bad about it and come runnin' the next morning to see if he was still alive and was so happy when he was. I remember them stories and some others. Grandma told 'em like they really happened, and some of 'em was hard to swallow, like the one where the three fellas was put in a fire and a fourth one appeared in the flames, and while he was there, they didn't burn. He saved 'em. Now, I kin hardly believe that happened, but it makes a rip of a story."

"Yes, it does." Ruth laughed softly at Mary's enthusiasm, and then she added plaintively, "In a way, it doesn't really matter if the story happened just like it's told. Stories teach us things. We face fire in our lives sometimes, and sometimes lions are around us, but through our faith we are protected. The fourth man in the fire was the Lord, Mary

Agatha. He saved the other three, and He can save us as well. That's what the story's saying, whether there really was a fiery furnace or not."

"Kin the Lord save you and Lucie?" the woman suddenly asked point-blank, her dark eyes glowing, and Ruth knew Mary understood more than just the literary lesson.

"Of course He can," said Ruth humbly, "and He will."

For more than an hour that first night Ruth read to "Skinny Agatha," the woman who scavenged for seeds and leaves and petals. She listened almost greedily, as if Ruth were possessed of magic, simply because she could decipher words on a page. And the words took on a luster themselves. Mary Agatha seemed to have no doubt they were from God. Certain verses from the Book of Mormon particularly intrigued her. Ruth saw that the woman was moved by what she heard.

Sensing that Mary was absorbing words and ideas into her very soul, Ruth turned to the second chapter of Jacob:

For behold, I, the Lord, have seen the sorrow, and heard the mourning of the daughters of my people in the land of Jerusalem, yea, and in all the lands of my people, because of the wickedness and abominations of their husbands. And I will not suffer, saith the Lord of Hosts, that the cries of the fair daughters of this people . . . shall come up unto me against the men of my people . . . for they shall not lead away captive the daughters of my people because of their tenderness, save I shall visit them with a sore curse . . . the sobbings of their hearts ascend up to God against you.

Mary Agatha listened intently to those words. Ruth repeated them and then added gently, "God grieves when His children are mistreated, especially His daughters, I believe. They are precious to Him."

"I want ya to read that to me again," said Mary Agatha. "I like the sounds of the words when you say 'em."

Lucie and I are captives of such cruelty, Ruth wanted to tell her, *but so are you, dear Mary.* Ruth wanted to say those words, but she held them back for now. She felt a new strength rising out of her own ability as a poet and a woman of faith. Could it be that she had found the way to Mary Agatha's heart? Had the eccentric woman, who

couldn't read, succumbed to the spell of enlightenment as if it were
an elixir sipped from her own supply? Ruth was intent and purposeful
with the scriptures she chose on the nights thereafter. She wanted
Mary Agatha to feel the Lord's love for His daughters. From Proverbs,
she read of the virtuous woman, hoping Mary Agatha would see
herself in the image: "*She seeketh wool, and flax, and worketh willingly
with her hands . . . She riseth also while it is yet night, and giveth meat
to her household . . . She stretcheth out her hand to the poor; yea, she
reacheth forth her hands to the needy.*" Mary Agatha's eyes glowed as she
heard those words, and she asked Ruth to read them over again.

From that first night on, Mary Agatha came to read and listen.
In the daytime, she went about her business, cooking, carrying water,
chopping wood, puttering among the flowering desert sage and
juniper, experimenting with her various potions on Lucie's wounds.
But at night she became a listener, enthralled by Ruth's clear voice
and the words she read. And slowly, almost imperceptibly, she began
to change. She was now sometimes more encouraging to Lucie.
"Your leg'll heal up in no time with this coneflower oil on it," she'd
say, although she was never really tender. She said nothing about Ez
Brackett's intentions. What happened to the girl in that regard merely
happened. It was the way of things, and Mary Agatha had no expe-
rience otherwise. But Ruth noted hopefully how the Lord's sorrow
over the mistreatment of women seemed to touch this unlikely
pupil, even if she could not yet see any application to herself. Men
took what they wanted when they wanted it in Mary Agatha's world,
and it would take more than a few hours of reading to change her
perspective.

Still, as the nights went by, as the words poured out of Ruth in
sonorous tones, Mary Agatha did seem affected, as if her hungering
soul had at last found nourishment in an unexpected place. One night,
after Ruth had gone through several passages simply for their beauty
and to perhaps direct her pupil's mind to new avenues of thought,
Ruth finally turned to the beginning of the Book of Mormon. "*I,
Nephi, having been born of goodly parents . . .*" Mary Agatha listened,
apparently engrossed—Lehi and his family traveling into the wilderness at the Lord's command to escape the evil in Jerusalem. She

remained silent throughout the first few chapters, perhaps thinking of her own desert wilderness and its challenges. Then came the episode involving Nephi's return to Jerusalem to acquire the record—the brass plates, which Laban had no intention of surrendering.

"You see how important these records were," Ruth pointed out. "The words of the Lord through His prophets are a treasure to always be preserved."

Mary Agatha nodded but said nothing. In the end, she seemed most struck by the surprising killing of Laban by the righteous Nephi, who first objected to the deed. *"Never at any time have I shed the blood of man. And I shrunk and would that I might not slay him,"* he recorded, but *"he had sought to take away mine own life."*

"He killed the man?" asked Mary Agatha when those verses were complete.

"Sometimes there's no other choice," replied Ruth. "Here, Nephi was authorized by the Lord to save something more important than one life—a nation that would dwindle in darkness without the records Laban had."

Mary Agatha looked doubtful. "This other book, the Bible, says, 'Thou shalt not kill.' I know it does."

"Yes, it does."

The woman looked at Ruth intently. "You wouldn't ever kill anyone, would ya?" she asked pointedly.

"No."

"Even if God told ya to, like He did that man?"

"I'm no Nephi," said Ruth. "I'll never hear the voice of God in that same way. And even if I did, I doubt I'd have the courage to believe it and carry through. I've used weapons to threaten people," she conceded. "Why, I threatened your Ez Brackett with a rifle when I had one. But it was only a threat. Killing isn't in me."

"No, it ain't. I kin tell that."

Ruth pondered a moment in silence. She felt that Mary Agatha was stirred by her presence and the words she had spoken and read. She sensed that the woman was looking at her in a new way, that Mary Agatha respected her and even loved her. The warmth of human affection flowed freely from one woman to the other.

"I can think of only one condition that would cause me to kill another person," Ruth mused, "the defense of my children. I would kill to protect any one of them, I think."

"You're a holy woman, Sister Ruth," said Mary Agatha. "Seems like killing *anyone* would taint yer soul somehow, even if ya had to do it."

The two women were seated on the floor of the cabin, framed by the darkness, their faces glowing in the candlelight. Above them in her makeshift bed, Lucie slept fitfully, whimpering softly at times, groaning a little at others. Ruth looked solemnly toward the bed and the young woman lying in it. "It might taint my soul, all right," she declared firmly, "but I'll tell you now; there's one other thing I'd cross that line for. If I can, I'll kill to save this girl." Looking Mary Agatha squarely in the eyes, Ruth added, "For some good reason, God placed me with Lucie, here and now. Like Nephi, I've been asked to face danger for a cause. I won't shrink from what might be required. Lucie's not my daughter, but she may as well be. They are all my children, the young women of the Church. I've been sent out to protect them."

Mary Agatha considered all of this thoughtfully, never taking her eyes from Ruth. Finally, she spoke with plainness. "You ain't got no way to kill Ez Brackett if it comes to that. A big man like him does as he pleases. What ya gonna do to stop anything he tries?"

"I don't know," replied Ruth miserably. "I have to have faith that God will provide a way."

"What ya need is a gun," said Mary Agatha abruptly, staring at Ruth.

Surprised, Ruth smiled a little. "Do you have such a thing?"

"No, I never had no want of one. The men do the huntin' around here. But I remember you was draggin' a rifle behind when ya first come." Mary raised a secretive eyebrow. "What become of that one ya had?"

"I don't know, and it wasn't loaded anyway. At least I don't think it was." Ruth hesitated. How trusting could she be of this woman? Of Ez Brackett's own relative? Perhaps, she worried, she had already said too much. Maybe Mary knew all about the gun and was merely testing her. A word from Mary Agatha, and Brackett would be on his guard about the rifle. Or was Mary Agatha sincere when she suggested the need for a gun? Ruth couldn't deny the bond of friendship that had been forged between them. Finally, her thoughts spilled out. "That rifle I brought in may have had one shell in the barrel. I don't know. And I don't know where it is. I passed out when I got here; when I woke up, the rifle was gone. I've looked for it in the lean-to and around the camp. Like I said, I'm not even certain it's loaded, but if I find it and can use it to help Lucie, I will."

"I still say sech a thing would taint yer soul," answered Mary plaintively. "Ya'd never be the same. Yer life weren't meant for killin'."

"It's Lucie that's important here, not me. I've lived my life, whatever it was meant for. I'll do what I have to. It's Lucie who counts now."

Mary Agatha smiled at Ruth's tenacity. It was a thin, mysterious smile that was covered in the shadows, and Ruth barely noticed it. But she hoped she was right about Mary Agatha. Cords of friendship, woven by mutual respect, were slowly tightening, and Nephi's words had fallen true on the woman's ears. *"But behold, I, Nephi, will show unto you that the tender mercies of the Lord are over all those whom he hath chosen, because of their faith, to make them mighty even unto the power of deliverance."* Ruth ached for that deliverance. They had been reading for six nights in a row by the time the gun was mentioned. David's sling? Nephi's sword? How much was Mary learning after all? There were now seven scratches on the cider barrel board, and Lucie's little calendar was black with all those days she'd marked to count the incremental steps toward some crucial resolution.

Chapter Eight
ISRAEL'S ARMY

FENTON MEADE MADE IT TO Modena some six hours after he left Ruth and Lucie at the wreckage site. Each of the twenty miles he rode was torture. He was forced to walk a good part of the way, having bounced from the horse twice, once into a gully of rough sand and brittlebrush and again when the animal shied at a rattlesnake in the road. Each mishap required Fenton to follow and catch the horse, and the second chase left him panting and exhausted a good distance from the trail. Lost in a wasteland of desert and sky, he found his path again only by giving the horse the lead and letting the gelding reach the familiar route on his own.

When a cluster of sheds and storefronts at last materialized on the horizon, Fenton was a shriveled figure, sunburned, grimy, and hollow-eyed. He had long since discarded his vest, and his shirt was covered with sand and sweat. He stumbled into the first building he came to, fell on his knees, and begged for water. It was half an hour before Fred Kane, the stationmaster at the rail stop, could make any sense of the fuzzy story about Tom Leavitt's carriage and the stranger on the road. "The northbound train has come and gone," the man told Fenton. "I wondered why the St. George freight never came." The stationmaster laid Fenton on a cot in his back room, and soon two other men were hovering over him asking questions. Fenton heard something about the telegraph being down or out of order. Then he drifted helplessly to sleep on the comfortable cot and heard nothing more.

***

The rail stop in Modena was a windswept outpost of clapboard, boasting only the depot and two stores. With the coming of the trains in 1899, Brigham J. Lund and his partners had invested in the place, building a mercantile and a saloon, but most California-bound travelers had no desire to linger in such a squalid oasis, and few got off the waiting trains long enough to browse or buy. Local residents were old-time wranglers or their wives, who drifted in from the outlying ranches when the work went dry. Some made a dollar selling trinkets—arrowheads and feathered beads—to stranded passengers. Others hoed backyard gardens and prayed for rain. The lucky ones worked for Lund at the mercantile or helped haul freight for the depot. There was no church in Modena. Local Mormons worshipped in Parowan or Cedar City or sometimes took the sacrament with a traveling bishop who was asked to oversee the dusty corners of Iron County where few people lived.

A rail line would someday reach St. George, but until then Modena teetered on the edge of the Utah desert, sending its trains on into Nevada—Pioche, Panaca, and beyond—taking travelers through a world of alkali, sagebrush, and desolate wilderness before California at last appeared on the horizon. Ezra Brackett spoke correctly when he talked with mocking venom about there being nothing in Modena. What, a posse of men to track him down? An army to surround him? Yes, Brackett knew Modena. But he failed to recognize the flintiness in Utah's men and the compelling fervor of a church that has lost one of its emissaries.

The next morning Fenton awoke to the smell of toast and bacon and hungrily ate the breakfast that was offered as he sat on the cot. A big fellow who introduced himself as James Colvin asked more questions, and suddenly Fenton became panic-stricken. "Oh, dear Lord," he cried, "Sister Ruth May Fox is stranded with that carriage!"

"What are you sayin'?" demanded Colvin, a former bishop. "First you tell us that Tom Leavitt's dead. Now you're sayin' that a lady from the general board is in trouble? Why didn't you tell us that when you first come in?"

"I tried," Meade groaned. "Please believe me. You've got to know I did my best. Please tell the Brethren I did my best. You've got to believe me."

"I believe you, son," said Bishop Colvin. "But I need you to tell me everything that happened, especially about the stranger."

Fenton started talking, breathlessly and in excited spurts. He told Colvin about Lucie Cole. "She's hurt," he said, "probably quite bad."

Colvin listened, yelling over his shoulder to the stationmaster at every pause. "That telegraph up yet?" and "When's the southbound due?" All the while he paced the planked floor and coaxed information out of the fear-stricken Fenton Meade. One of Fred Kane's baggage boys was dispatched to an outlying ranch where the town's only "doctor" lived. The man, Robert Morgan, wasn't certified, but he was the nearest thing Modena had to a medical practitioner, having attended to bullet wounds, broken bones, and five kinds of mountain fever during his long life on the prairie. When he at last saw Fenton, rest and nourishment were all he could prescribe, knowing, with Shakespeare, that in many cases "the patient must minister to himself."

"This boy's biggest problem is anxiety," Morgan told Colvin, "and if what he says is true, no one can blame him for that. Tom Leavitt dead. Two women left in the desert with a madman on the loose? Why, that's enough to terrorize us all."

But darkness had settled on Modena before anything else could be accomplished.

"Won't do any good to go off half-cocked," said Colvin while he paced, and when Kane at last informed him that the telegraph was "sparking," he directed a message to St. George and to Cedar City informing authorities of the emergency. By morning, a return message had come from Elder Jennings Burton, a General Authority. "Bound from Cedar in haste. Hold rescue posse until I arrive."

"Dang! St. George sheriff is gonna beat us to it," complained Colvin, but he waited dutifully for Burton and used the time to assemble his men.

Only a few families lived in Modena, but outlying ranches had their share of wranglers and hired roustabouts. Colvin was amazed at

how quickly word of the emergency spread. Before 9 a.m., two men
from the Pecos Verde had appeared and then three more from a ranch
near the Nevada line. He explained the situation with as much detail
as he could and then paced again as he waited impatiently for Burton.
When the southbound train arrived at 9:30, two detectives, Ray
Sherman and Dean Kellihue, got off and offered their services. They
had received a telegram from Salt Lake during their routine stop in
Delta. The Church was putting its best security on the case.

Elder Burton pulled up before noon in a covered carriage with
an aide and the Cedar City sheriff, John Frazier. Burton was a solidly
built man in his forties, a farm boy–turned-businessman before his
call to the presiding bishopric of the Church. He knew Ruth May
Fox and her husband, Jesse, well, and he'd already personally wired
the family. "Jesse and a couple of the boys wanted to catch the next
train," he told Colvin. "I told them to hold off until I had a better
idea of what was going on. Let's have good news for them by the time
they get down here. The Church will contact the Cole family as well."
He and Frazier talked to Fenton Meade and gave the young man a
priesthood blessing. Burton was solicitous, thanking Fenton for his
"heroic" efforts and assuring him that he was in no way slack in his
duty. But he remarked to Frazier as they left, "Perhaps we need to
take another look at who we send out with our women."

The two detectives, Sherman and Kellihue, also questioned
Meade then coordinated their plans with Colvin, Frazier, and Burton.
By 1:30 the entire party was ready to depart into the wilderness along
the southbound road. Frazier and Burton drove a spring wagon lined
with blankets and stocked with food, water, and the few medical
supplies they'd been able to muster. The other men, eight in all,
rode their own horses and moved ahead of the wagon. Dr. Morgan
followed in his own buggy but at a considerably slower pace.

Colvin hoped to arrive at the wreckage site before the St.
George authorities, but he knew that time, if not distance, was on
Washington County's side. Patch Booker, the St. George sheriff, had
to cover about forty-five miles to Colvin's twenty, but Booker had
undoubtedly started at first light. "Danged if I'm gonna let a thug

from Iron County cause damage to the Church or its fine sisters," breathed Colvin to himself, "and Frazier can back me there."

As it turned out, Booker and his men had rummaged through the wreckage for half an hour before the first horses from Modena came upon them. Patch Booker was still shaking his head over finding Tom Leavitt's body. "Known him all my life," he said. "I sure never figured on anything like this."

The reality of the scattered wreckage in the wash and seeing Leavitt dead confirmed Fenton's story and cast a pall over the rescuers. Two women had vanished into the desert, where their chances of survival were slim. Whether they were hostages of a crazed man or merely wandering on their own, Colvin and the others were suddenly weighted down with apprehension. They spoke only in whispers and short sentences, but the fear was palatable. Even as they sorted through the remains of Ruth's obvious attempt at helping Lucie—the shaded resting place, the discarded pieces of torn clothing—hope eluded them. A weary foreboding lined their faces. This was serious business, with one good man already lost. Then they found Brackett's red bandana on the post at one end of the gully, and it seemed another sign that danger lay ahead. They left the bandana there, drooping on the post, to mark the site and serve as a reminder of the suffering the gully had posed for those they loved.

Booker had decided to wait for the party from Modena before moving Leavitt's body. Once the detectives had examined the site, he'd send Tom home in a wagon with a proper escort. Tom would be sorely missed.

Jennings Burton was sobered by what he saw. Ruth Fox was his friend and colleague. Her husband and sons were at that moment anxiously waiting to head south, and Jennings dreaded facing them with desperate news. "We've got to find these women," he told Booker. "At least there's hope. They're not in this gully, sharing Mr. Leavitt's fate."

Booker scanned the desert with narrow eyes. "We don't yet know for sure about their fate, Brother Burton. But you're right. At least they didn't meet it here."

The General Authority vowed to not give up. When one of the local ranchers approached the wagon and suggested that Burton aim his glasses toward the cluster of rocky hills due west, he was anxious to oblige. "A group of outcasts roams that boulder country over there," said the man. "*Spirit chasers* is what we call 'em, 'cause they seem to be some religious band or cult. We don't see much of 'em, 'cept when they come out to steal. Nothing big. A chicken, maybe, or a discarded tool or saddle. It's never been worth the trouble of tracking them down—that's wild country where they hide."

Burton searched the western foothills with his field glasses and then jumped down from the wagon, walking with the rancher and John Frazier several yards in that direction. The prairie winds, which spread the sand like fine dust, had already blown away the tracks of the travois, except in the few places where the ground was damp and pasty from the water Ruth had sacrificed. Even these spots were scarce after more than two days of dry breezes, but some were shaded by clumps of scrub and sage, and after an hour of crossing back and forth over the area, Frazier found what he thought were hoof prints and a double furrow headed west. Then, the rancher saw a sticky crust of salt on one of the scrub leaves. Taking it in his fingers, he tasted it and shouted to the others about his find.

Soon more telltale signs were discovered, and in some places the salt remained in Ruth's moist footprints. The white crystals led the searchers forward, and by the time the trail of salt had run its course, the men were half a mile from where they started with something more than wild guesses to lead them. They scanned the distant foothills now with renewed hope.

"One thing we got going for us," said Burton. "Ruth May Fox is sharp as a tailor's needle and always has her wits about her. If she's not injured, both women have a chance."

Still, the horizon was baffling, a vast panorama of sky and waste-land studded by chimneys of rock. Shifting dunes left even the local men confused about directions. Trying desperately to set some kind of worthwhile course, Burton called the men together in a circle. There they prayed, importuning heaven for the guidance they needed and listening for the still small voice.

Burton had everyone sit around him, and with a stick he drew a rough outline of the topography he saw directly to the west, each ridge and hump of boulders, each shadowy draw or canyon. All were laid out in the sand as they appeared against the sky. "The perspective will change as we move closer," Burton reminded them, "but another man stood on this spot a few days ago and chose his route based on what we're seeing now. Which way did he go and why? We need to come to some reckoning about it and then take that trail."

A narrow divide to the right on Burton's outline seemed to be a worthwhile possibility. "A wedge like that means there's a trail or maybe a creek of some kind," said Colvin. "My guess is they're camped somewhere up behind those hills."

"But you've got another canyon up here to the left," offered Frazier, using a stick to point out what he meant then waving it toward the horizon as he looked west. "That draw would just as likely lead to some box canyon back behind."

"I've chased stray cows up that draw," one of the ranchers put in. "There's nothing there but fireweed and yuccas and not much of that. No water at all, though the cows think they can smell it."

"That draw to the right is a far piece as well," added Colvin. "We got to guess that someone was walking or maybe being dragged along on a travois, judging by the tracks. Distance would be a problem."

"If that's where your home is, that's where you go," shrugged Booker. "Don't matter how far it is."

"Maybe we should split up," suggested Colvin. "There are a dozen of us. Six can head in each direction until someone finds a solid trail."

In the end, they looked to Jennings Burton, the highest-ranking priesthood holder present. Even Sherman and Kellihue, the Church detectives, deferred to him, believing as they did in his calling. Burton listened to what each man had to say and, after pondering the outlined map before him, pointed his stick to the first wedge on the right. "We won't split up," said Burton. "If it's a camp of people, we'll need every man. Whenever we find Ruth and Lucie, it's likely we'll need the wagon and the doctor. It's best to stay together." He shoved his stick upright into the chosen wedge to affirm the decision. "We'll go here," he said.

Marching back to the wreckage to gather up their horses and supplies, they were soon moving as one body in the direction Burton had decreed. But the desert worked against them. Distances were farther than they seemed. It took the troop two full days to cross the valley and find an expected source of water. The men were slow to rise on the third morning. The stream was eventually found as they drew closer to the foothills, but by then exhaustion hobbled them, and they were forced to spend another night on the range without much progress for their effort. Worse than any hardship was the fact that there was nothing to be found, not a footprint, not a fire pit, not one sure sign that anyone had crossed this way.

On the afternoon of the fourth day, the wind lifted up like Satan's broom, and the men were forced to grab onto their hats and cover their faces to avoid the rising dust. They sought shelter in a dry gully, much like the one they had left four days before but more shallow and less likely to flood. Billowing dark clouds in the northwest signaled the approaching storm, and occasional sparks of lightning skipped along the mountains. "The devil's cursing at us," said Colvin, "daring us to come in his direction."

Within minutes, the sky opened like a sieve and torrents of rain began plastering the gully and soaking everything. Large drops fell in clusters whipped about by the wind, and soon every swale or gully bottom was flooded and pasty mud seeped down the edges of the wash. The posse left the gully, fearful lest a flash flood swamp them. Several of the men crawled under the spring wagon to wait out the cloudburst; others pulled the top on the doctor's buggy and huddled beneath it. "We don't get 'em too often in these parts," remarked one of the ranchers, "but when they come it's like yer troubles, 'not as single spies, but in battalions.'"

"It'll be a fight for the horses to struggle through the mud," said Colvin. "Be up to their knees in spots, I reckon."

"Once the rain lets up, we'll have to wait until the sand dries out a little," mused Burton, "but I hate to put things off too long." His eyes searched the western edge of the sky, smudged now like a chalky illustration blurred from being left out in the rain. "We have to hope that the women have found safe shelter," he added. "Like us, they're waiting out the storm."

As the pelting rain splashed about them and ran in rivulets down the sides of the wagon, James Colvin took the opportunity to talk soberly to the General Authority next to him. He had never met a member of Church hierarchy before, and he was deferential in the presence of the man. "I'm ashamed we let this happen in our county," he told Burton. "Ruth May Fox is loved here. I know that for a fact. A woman on Church business is the Lord's own angel. I have faith that He'll look after her until we, as His servants, can do our part to find her."

Burton nodded as he pensively watched the rain. "I'm convinced Ruth put herself in danger for the sake of Lucie Cole," he said. "It's something she would do."

"Do you know the lady well?" asked Colvin.

"We're in the same ward at home. Her husband is our block teacher. He's a good man, Jesse Fox, very supportive of his wife."

"Children at home?"

"Oh, yes, several. The older ones have gone, but there must be five or six still under Jesse's roof, the youngest still a child who needs her mother."

"The Brethren know best," said Colvin with some hesitation, "but it can be risky for a woman traveling far from home."

"You don't know Ruth May Fox." Burton smiled softly. "We couldn't hold her back if we wanted to. She'd go anywhere. She's a comet when it comes to laboring for the kingdom, full of fire and light. Do you know, Colvin," he added after a minute, musing over the dreary scene before them, "they say we'll fly someday. I've heard that engineers are working on air machines right now, even as we talk. I don't doubt that it will happen, and I'll tell you this: if there ever is a way to fly, Ruth May Fox will do it. She came to Utah walking, but there will come a time when she'll serve Zion with silver wings, like the angel that she is."

There was a faraway gleam in Burton's eye, and Colvin took the words as prophecy, though he personally didn't put much stock in aeroplanes flying very far. What he worried over was the here and now. Burton's prophecy would never be fulfilled if the desert swallowed Ruth May Fox before Israel's army found her.

Under the doctor's buggy, Kellihue was having another kind of conversation with one of the St. George deputies, a fellow named Bodis Smith. "What can you tell me about this sect we're looking for? Are they a violent bunch?"

"They're petty thieves," said Smith. "I've never feared violence from them till today. I've known Tom Leavitt for years, since he began runnin' freight. Seein' him dead like that kinda jolts a fellow. You know what I mean?"

Kellihue watched the rain dripping from their makeshift roof beneath the buggy. "We haven't put things all together yet. It might have been an accident that killed the driver."

"No, there's more to it than that. And it makes me fear a-mighty for those women. The elder there says Ruth May Fox is a strong, independent sort that don't take no guff from nobody. I fear for her if that's the truth, 'cause these spirit chasers are hard on their women." Smith hesitated, and when Kellihue remained silent, he added, "I've never seen much of 'em—the spirit chaser women, I mean—but the time or two I have, they look weak and beaten down, pale and glassy-eyed as wounded sparrows, and they didn't get that way from being overfed and pampered."

"Sister Fox may be strong and independent," said Kellihue, "but she's also very smart. She'll know how to handle trouble. It's the girl's situation that could change things, and that's what worries me—and probably worries Ruth. She'll put herself in harm's way for that girl. I know she will. That's why we've got to find them soon, before things get out of hand."

Smith nodded. Then he looked out at the soaking rain and the sodden prairie with its miles of empty waste, and he wondered if they were already too late.

For three more days the men accomplished nothing. The heavy showers were intermittent, but the trail was a sloppy river of sand and mud even during patches of clear weather. They could see black clouds smothering the mountains ahead of them and knew the storm still ruled the canyons there.

"God, give Ruth shelter," Jennings Burton prayed every night, "and the young woman who is with her, Lucie Cole."

Chapter Nine
SOLACE IN THE STORM

THE SAME DELUGE THAT DRENCHED Burton's men flooded the scattered remains of Tom Leavitt's freight wagon and all its scattered refuse. A day later, the worst of it spilled down on Ruth's crude roof as well, pelting the spirit chasers' hideaway even as Burton and his men were mopping up. Ruth and Lucie's little cabin leaked under its eaves in one corner and shook at every thunderclap. Lightning flashes lit up the windowless room like a lantern's beam because of the holes. Ruth used containers from the medicinal shelf to catch the rain and tried to stuff the largest holes with rags. Water seeped beneath the door and under the wooden slats that made up the floor. Ruth pressed rolled pieces of her quilt tightly around the frame and stuffed the cracks with a woolen shawl Mary Agatha had left, but the fix was only temporary, for the fabric was soon soaked through. The cabin was an ugly shack at best, but it must have outlasted many bouts with violent weather before.

And for all the damage and discomfort it brought, Ruth felt insulated by the storm. While it raged outside, ravaging the camp, leaving every loose kettle floating in a fire pit and broken branches littering the ground, it drove the enemy away and the predator back into its hole. Ez Brackett was nowhere to be seen throughout the drizzling afternoon, and even Mary Agatha, trudging up the path under a dirty cloak, stayed only long enough to help Ruth lift Lucie out of bed to be washed and helped with her personal needs. Mary brought two dry quilts, protected by the overlap of her cloak across her arm. Where Mary had gotten them, Ruth couldn't guess, but the thought crossed her mind that the woman might have given up her own bedding to keep Ruth and Lucie warm. The woman was eager to leave quickly, escaping any questions.

The floor was wet and slippery, and Ruth spent a good deal of time wiping up and trying to plug the worst of the leaks. She emptied the chamber pot and covered all of Mary's herbs and salves with a flimsy rug before the rain left them floating on the shelf. "No fire outside tonight," she murmured, "not tomorrow either unless they keep the kindling dry." Ruth had wanted to ask Mary about where the others were. Clara and Gertie and Royal Jacobs and especially Brackett. There were seven slashes on the cider barrel board, and Ruth knew he'd be growing impatient.

"Ezra goes up in the big cave by the mesa when it storms," Mary Agatha had told her once. "So do most of the others, all scurryin' for shelter on a rainy night. It's dry enough to shrivel a cornstalk in that cave. The women like it 'cause they ain't no work once the cookin's done. The men kin smoke and palaver all they want. They'll drink a quart a whiskey and start seein' stars and visions 'fore the night is out, and one or two of 'em will begin to speak in tongues. It used to be Ez that done it, but he's turned sour as a pickle vat since his woman died. Not that he ever did much for her 'cept crack the whip. Now he's all wrought up inside over this poor gal 'cause her leg's broke and he has to wait for what he wants. Ez never was no good at waitin', I kin tell ya that."

Alone now, Ruth stole a glance at Lucie. Mary Agatha had hurried away, and it was probably for the best. They didn't need the woman's blunt, unschooled rhetoric tonight. But when Ruth thought about the dry quilts and Mary's possible sacrifice, she softened. Suddenly, she felt renewed concern for this strange, erstwhile reading companion. Ruth had watched as Mary wrapped the dirty cloak around herself and turned to brave the rain. "Will *you* be dry tonight, dear Mary?" Ruth asked quite simply. "Is there a cave for you?"

Mary Agatha had stepped back from the door, a little startled. "Oh, ya," she said at last, "my dugout's deep and cozy. I won't be bothered there." She paused again. "Ya know, Sister Ruth, I don't remember anyone ever callin' me 'dear Mary.' The sound is odd to me, but I know you meant well, all the same."

She left then, and Ruth watched her go, trudging down the wet path and vanishing into the shadows.

"She's never been called 'dear Mary'?" Lucie spoke softly from the bed. "I can hardly believe . . . such a simple thing."

Ruth looked from Lucie to the door and back again. "Kindness, and even courtesy, is so lacking in her life," she said, "even the sound was unfamiliar. And yet, Mary Agatha herself sometimes treats others with selflessness if not compassion. Have you noticed that?"

Lucie nodded, and Ruth continued musing to herself about strange Mary Agatha. It was as if some gifts came naturally with no specific instruction or example. They revealed themselves unvarnished, unrefined, but only occasionally in the midst of more rough-hewn habits.

With her lantern, Ruth moved to Lucie's bed to help her in, tucking the blanket around her and pulling the pillow up behind. Lucie's sad eyes followed her as she worked, and when Ruth finished and took Lucie's hand, tears welled up again in the girl's eyes. Lucie's dark hair hung to her shoulders, and Ruth tenderly touched a stray lock of it, combing it back with her fingers. "Surely, those aren't tears I'm seeing," said Ruth, curving her lip into a half smile. "We're safe tonight, dear Lucie, even from the rain."

"It's not that." Lucie looked into Ruth's face. The girl yearned for answers, Ruth could tell, answers and affirmation. Finally she continued. "I know what will probably happen here." Then her eyes met Ruth's again. "You've been so kind, so protective, so selfless in my behalf. Mary's goodwill might come in spurts, but yours is constant, Sister Fox. I don't know why we two came to face this terror together, and I certainly mean you no ill will. But I'm grateful that you're here with me, if these things had to be."

She squeezed Ruth's hand and placed the other one across her wrist, and Ruth looked into her eyes. "Don't lose hope, Lucie," she said. "Good men will find us, even here. Angels will show them the way."

For several seconds Lucie remained still. Ruth listened to her breathe, kept hold of her hand, and waited, knowing she was not asleep. The lantern candle flickered in the shadows. The rain on the roof tapped steadily, like the meter of a poem. Ruth was warm with a spiritual reverie when Lucie finally spoke again. "Will Albert feel differently toward me, Sister Fox, if I come back to him unpure?"

Ruth hesitated and then answered gently but without equivocation. "Purity is a condition of the soul, dear Lucie, not the body. Jesus said, 'Blessed are the pure in heart.' Surely your Albert knows that too. The Lord looketh upon the heart and the intent of our hearts in spite of circumstances we can't control."

"You're being kind, Sister Fox, but perhaps not realistic as the world judges things."

"The world judges as it will," Ruth answered. "It's our Heavenly Father who judges all. Purity is a virtue, Lucie, and virtue can't be stolen. It's not a silver coin at the bottom of a purse for thieves to snatch. Virtue dwells in a righteous heart, and no one can trespass there."

Ruth's words seemed to comfort Lucie. Her eyes glowed in the candlelight. "Why did you follow us, Sister Fox? Why did you follow Brackett and the travois across the desert? You could be safe now in Modena and told the rescuers where to look for me. Instead, you followed. And now you're here, eating mush and weeds, sleeping on the dirty floor, and who knows what will become of either of us?"

"Don't you worry about me," said Ruth. "I came south on the Lord's errand. A thousand girls to serve or only one—I'm exactly where I'm supposed to be."

"Still, your devotion to the one may cost the others more than they deserve to lose," Lucie whispered. "I wouldn't want to be responsible for that, as much as I've needed you. I feel guilty about it—you being in all this trouble because of me."

"Nonsense, Lucie. We're in trouble because of Ezra Brackett."

The sound of the raindrops on the roof seemed to share the rhythm of Ruth's heart. Nature seemed to be weeping for them as they huddled in the little hut.

Ruth reached forward to straighten Lucie's pillow and look her in the eye. "Listen to me," she said. "Your virtue is yours to keep whatever happens, but I still don't want you hurt. And you won't be, as long as I have breath."

"What can you do?"

"The Brethren are coming. I know they are. In the meantime, there's a Henry rifle somewhere that I haven't forgotten about. I had it when I came. Brackett doesn't think it's loaded, so it's probably just lying around. If I can find it, we might have something to bluff or bargain with. But don't you worry, Lucie. You'll be all right."

Ruth slid from the side of the bed and to the bottom until her back was against the wall. Her small shoulders were erect; her chin was up. The rain dripped off the eaves outside and leaked through at the corners, but Ruth was absorbed again in the rhythm of the sound. As she sat at the bottom of the bed, contemplating Lucie in the shadows, her words came softly. "Do you really want to know why I followed you? Do you want to know why I'm here?"

Lucie didn't answer, but Ruth knew that she was listening.

"I have a daughter with your name, as I've told you," Ruth continued. "Lucy Beryl. She's thirteen now, all braids and brown eyes. She's not my only daughter—or my only child, heaven knows! But I want to tell you a story about Lucy that may be meaningful to you, since you share her name." Ruth settled herself a little as her thoughts began to coalesce. The rain harmonized with her words as she began her tale, and Lucie felt that she had never heard a voice so beautiful.

"A few months before Lucy Beryl was born, I saw her in a dream. She was a young woman in the vision, but I knew her. I knew she was my child who even then was growing in my womb. We walked together through a beautiful garden in a world too exquisite to describe. Nature was all about us—flowers, trees, green mountain slopes, and airy mists of loveliness like great painters can produce—and there was a touch of mystery too, as if so much more was being hidden from my eyes because I was mortal and so unprepared. The young woman radiated goodness. She took my hand, and at her touch I was filled with spiritual fire, an affirmation I cannot explain.

I asked her if she knew me, and she nodded and embraced me and said she knew she would be coming to mortality soon and that I was the mother who would welcome her. But she was troubled too and begged me to listen to her sorrows.

"She was sad about leaving the peace and beauty around her?" asked Lucie.

"It was more than that. She seemed to have a prescience or fore-sight about what lay ahead. In some kind of heavenly transformation, I was swept along into her ethos, and as my dream deepened, that world became familiar to me, as if I'd once been part of it myself. My Lucy Beryl already knew her brothers and her sisters. I'd lost a child, Eliza, years before, and Lucy knew her. She knew her father and me. She knew much about the status of our Zion and of the world outside our mountains. She was so afraid . . . afraid of what mortality required. Suffering and bitterness, the loss of loved ones, the possibil-ity of failure, our vulnerability to sin. In my dream my Lucy wept and begged me to somehow shield her from such pain, which of course I could not do. Still, for the first time as we talked, I realized just how courageous we all once were to brave this mortal journey."

"What did you tell her?" breathed Lucie through the darkness. "How did you dry her tears?"

"I told her that Christ Jesus bore our sorrows and that our faith would see us through."

"Was she comforted?" said Lucie, knowing the same message belonged to her.

"Yes," answered Ruth, "but my dream did not end there. My Lucy Beryl showed me the future, *my* future in the Church. Suddenly, she was not just my Lucy anymore but every girl and woman in my dream—a million of them reaching out as she had for sustenance and strength. I learned my calling, Lucie. I saw myself in far-off lands and in the islands of the sea, speaking, preaching, nurturing the young women of the Church. At times I felt like I was flying, though I don't know how, and always Lucy Beryl's spirit traveled with me. My connection to her was never broken though I soared far away—sometimes earthbound, sometimes not—and heard the songs I knew, sung by voices from across the globe."

"You heard them because you wrote them, Sister Fox. I know you're a poet."

"I dabble," said Ruth modestly. "I love the written word, especially as it pertains to the gospel. I've often cried like Alma, '*O that I were an angel, and could have the wish of mine heart, that I might go forth and speak with the trump of God . . .*'" Ruth laughed a little. "O that I were a *writer* and could have the wish of mine heart . . . and speak with the trump of God. That's what I always say. So I dabble with gospel poems and hope the 'trump' is in there somewhere."

Ruth moved to the edge of the bed, and her feet slipped to the floor. There she stood looking down at the girl's face in the shadows, and at last she took Lucie's hand. "That dream I had pierced my soul," she whispered, "and gave me an intense emotional connection with my Lucy and all the Lucys, Anns, and Rachels of the Church, all young women of every name. My mission is to them. They are vulnerable in this mortal world, as you are, injured here in this cabin with evil threatening at the door. But I will stand by them—and I will stand by you—until the Savior and His gospel bring us safely home."

"Say one of your poems to me," murmured Lucie. "I'm afraid, like the Lucy in your dream. Say a poem that comforts me as you once comforted her."

Ruth dropped to the edge of the bed again. The sound of the rain outside had turned from a heavy rhythm to a string of leftover notes, and the thunder was dying in weak echoes along the western peaks. Lucie was almost asleep, drifting away under the spell of Ruth's words. Lovingly, Ruth repeated something she had written long before as a young woman adjusting to a new home, a new marriage, and all the challenges of life. It was about the faith that had always been her shelter in the worst of storms.

The gospel is the purist light that travels from afar.
'Tis kindled nigh to Kolob
Like sun and morning star.

Its fire covers all the world, from seas to prairie sod.
It casts a constant perfect beam,
Its source, the love of God.

And though it's born of heavenly fire and divine celestial spark,
It's as earthbound as a hearthstone,
Or a streetlamp in the dark.

It's a match struck by a stranger, wherever wand'rers roam,
Or a candle in the window
That marks the pathway home.

It lights the eye,
It fires the soul,
It keeps the child warm.
It offers a torch in the blackest night,
And solace in the storm.

Lucie was fully asleep by the time Ruth finished the poem, and the poetess was pleased that it had done its work.

Chapter Ten
FIRM AS THE MOUNTAINS AROUND US

RUTH MADE IT A POINT never to leave Lucie alone. However, she knew that both of them needed exercise, movement, and fresh air. She and Mary Agatha had managed to lift Lucie up to a standing position early on, and they encouraged her to "walk" about with her weight on their shoulders not too long after that. With their help, she managed well, keeping the broken leg stiff and above the floor. "We don't want bed sores," said Mary, "and she needs to work her other limbs. Don't do no good to lay about."

At first, Lucie had been reluctant. She was still bruised and broken and in some pain in spite of Mary Agatha's saps and potions. But she was also anxious to move, to get out of bed, out of the hut, to be aggressive in helping Ruth find a way out of this crisis. Sometimes Lucie's heart pounded, and her body shivered uncontrollably. The heat of panic would pass over her like a sudden fever, leaving her cold and clammy after it was gone. But movement and purpose seemed to help fend off the anxiety, and Ruth could see improvement in Lucie's outlook.

"It feels good to be straight up again," she said during one of her walks outside the cabin, "even if I am hopping on one foot." Lucie knew humor was important too and strived to maintain some sense of it.

"You'll dance with Albert at your wedding," said Ruth stoutly and watched the girl inhale the mountain breezes, her face and hair shining in the sunlight once again. Ah, the resilience of youth. This girl was in grave danger, yet she was keeping faith with that optimistic spirit that promised the ultimate blessing and positive result. Ruth admired her for that, for it was a virtue she had lived her life to teach, to bequeath, and in her own way, to exemplify.

On Lucie's other side, Mary Agatha held her stiffly and listened to Ruth encourage her. "It's good she's as little as she is," Mary mused to Ruth. "I had to pull Gertie Royal out of a cow slime once and thought I'd break my back doin' it."

The day after the storm, when puddles filled every low-lying ditch and crevice and when downed tree limbs were scattered about, Ruth joined the other women in clearing the refuse, earning the grudging respect of Clara Tophorn, Gertie Royal, and Tessie Grover as she worked to make the little village somewhat livable again. Keeping one eye on the hut where Lucie waited, she and Mary Agatha chopped all the broken wood to use for kindling, rescued pots and pans from muddy fire pits, and reconstructed clotheslines and lean-to doors that had been damaged by the storm. "You're an able worker for your size," said Gertie Royal to Ruth as they shoveled away the mud that had clogged one end of the spring. "And there's willingness in yer soul. I'll give ya that."

Mary Agatha suddenly moved between the two women as if she were protecting Ruth from some evil swarm of bees. "You git on outa here, Gertie," she screeched. "Sister Ruth don't need your palaverin'!"

Gertie chortled foolishly through her missing teeth and moved farther down the stream. Ruth looked at Mary Agatha with surprise. "It's all right. She was giving me a compliment. She meant no harm."

"Harm is all that Gertie Royal knows," Mary Agatha snorted. "She'd grin wide while she slit yer throat and laugh about it after."

"Surely not," said Ruth, smiling and chalking up Mary Agatha's action to a bit of possessiveness. She had definitely built a bond with Mary Agatha with her reading and teaching and constant concern for Lucie. But whether it was an affinity that foretold good or ill, Ruth could not yet guess.

It was the eighth day, and the men had disappeared, leaving most of the labor to the women of camp with the excuse that several horses and other animals had been scattered by the thunder and needed to be rounded up. Some had even made it through the slot and were wandering on the rocky hills below. Ruth saw more likely reasons for the men leaving. The cleaning of the camp simply did not concern Ez and his companions, and they jumped at the first excuse to ride down the canyon and leave the mess behind. *More importantly, they're keeping an eye out for our rescuers,* Ruth thought and felt some kind of climax coming now that the storm had passed. Surely, the posse had been hindered by the storm, which had drained the sky for three days and counting. Surely that was the reason the rescuers had not appeared. Now, with the morning bright and the sky cloudless, they would come en masse, like Israel's army, to save her and Lucie.

There were eight scratches on the cider barrel board before they'd finished breakfast and begun the cleanup. Clara Tophorn took it upon herself to carve the latest slash, knowing the men were not expected until dusk. "My Cal has a dog in this fight," she laughed as she scraped the blade along the wood. "He don't believe Ez can leave the girl alone ten days. Two more, an' it won't matter." Ruth looked on ruefully, hoping Lucie would never see the cider barrel board or ask about its ugly marks.

The eighth day. It was part hope and part curiosity that led Ruth to follow Mary Agatha that afternoon up a craggy bluff where the medicine woman claimed there would be a fresh blossoming of prickly pear cactus with its yellow flowers and its pads, good for poultices once they were peeled. Prickly pears were found clustered on the desert floor, but they also flourished in level spaces above draws and ridges. Mary Agatha said she hoped to find fireweed too and perhaps some hemlock if she was lucky. Ruth felt that Lucie would be safe for a few hours without her. The men were gone, and Lucie urged her to make the hike, silently recognizing Ruth's main purpose. Perhaps, with a good view of the valley, Ruth would see where the expected rescue riders were and which way they were headed. Perhaps there would be some way to signal them or persuade Mary Agatha that they were about to be swarmed by officers of the law and she may as well choose the winning side. Ruth's nerves were as raw as the scratches on the cider barrel board, and though Lucie didn't know about the wager, she too sensed time running out. Some kind of resolution was about to come, be it rescue or defeat, and if Ruth could get a clear view of anything . . .

"I'll be all right here," Lucie told her. "You go see what you can find."

Ruth caught the double meaning and squeezed Lucie's arm before she followed Mary Agatha out the door, giving the girl the Book of Mormon to read and a parting nod of reassurance. She'd see what she could find all right, and hopefully it would be more than cactus thorns and stinging nettle.

Mary Agatha, with a large sowing sack over her shoulder, led Ruth down the trail and out of the slot canyon which obscured the camp. The tall ungainly woman had to almost double up as she moved through the winding slot. Ruth walked behind her, wondering if she could ever get Lucie to the bottom by this route. Not without help, she knew, and the thought depressed her. Once out of the canyon, they found their route and struggled to the path that would lead them to the top of the highest bluff.

As their steps ranged upward through the flat boulders and thistle-grown crevices above, Mary Agatha fashioned a walking stick from a cedar branch and handed it to her companion. Her own bony shoulders were hunched over slightly, and she was in need of something to lean on herself, but she clung doggedly to the path, knowing precisely where she was going.

Ruth moved with some enthusiasm, proud of the fact that at nearly fifty years old, she could still walk a mountain path and keep up with a woman who was far more used to physical exertion. It demonstrated, too, that her wounds and bruises were healing. This hike was far less daunting than her torturous walk behind Ez Brackett's horse, and that fact represented progress. She had always taken pride in progressing, moving forward even in the worst of times, and her life had been a portrait of that determination.

She had viewed herself as simply a bearer of glad tidings and affection to all the young women and their leaders. She yearned to nourish these good people with the power of the gospel principles she taught, inspired by the foresight she possessed that someday the work would fill the earth. She followed Mary Agatha now, hoping for a different kind of vision, one of rescue and succor in a lonely Utah desert. As she climbed, she viewed the barren wilderness below and tried to find some hopeful sign that even here glory and justice would prevail.

Mary Agatha began collecting any bloom she found in the crevices along the way—fireweed, shepherd's purse, flowering juniper. Small prickly pear cactus pads flourished in the dry soil where the blazing sun was inescapable. Other plants sought the shaded crevices of rocks and overhangs, or they wedged themselves into the low areas where rainwater collected. Each one was a treasure for Mary Agatha, and she fondled the petals and leaves carefully before placing them in her bag. "The tea from these is good for coughs and sometimes growling stomachs," she told Ruth. "Others make good poultices. They heal by drawing the poison out of wounds, and they kin slow down bleeding. They're a gift from nature, to be sure."

Ruth nodded and helped gather certain thistle blooms she found, being careful not to sting her fingers. "Where did you learn about all this?" she asked Mary Agatha. "How did you happen on to what you know?"

"There was an Indian woman taught me some of it when we first come west. The tribes used to roam these hills more than they do now. They're all tied to the reservation down south, the Paiute and the Shivwits, but we used to see 'em often, and I had a chance to learn their ways. It's always been an interest for me, how seeds and saps and nettles mixed up together can have healing powers. I've always been one to try things out, stir around a bit, and see what happens. There seems to be a magic to it, and that keeps me at my work, I reckon."

"You have the mind to be a real doctor," said Ruth admiringly, "or perhaps a chemist whose discoveries help fight disease. Folks like you are a marvel, Mary Agatha, and your life's been wasted in this desert." Ruth bit her tongue at those last words. She was grateful that Mary was in the desert now—for Lucie's sake and her own.

Mary Agatha was fumbling with a bunch of thistles and took no offense. "Doctorin' ain't known to be women's work in cities like yours. I suppose I do more doctorin' here than I ever would anywheres else."

"Well, that's not exactly true," argued Ruth, slipping down to lean against a smooth ledge and peer into the valley. "We Saints have our women doctors. Ellis Shipp and Martha Hughes Cannon are famous for their practices. Both of them went east for education and came back to serve Zion with their skills. It was found that we women prefer women doctors, especially during childbirth."

Mary Agatha looked up from her work. "I know a lot about bringing a baby," she said proudly. "Them two kids of Clara's? I brung both of 'em, and both times Clara set up a fuss, squealin' like she was an old sow trapped in a mud wallow. There was no men to help hold her down, neither, or do nuthin' else to help. But Clara pushed and I pulled, and together we got the slippery little beggars into the world. I slapped their bottoms good and hard till they sang out loud. It was a pleasin' sound and the only time ya pray to hear a child scream."

Ruth moved ahead along the path, climbing higher than she'd intended, struggling until her bruised shoulder ached again and her ribs were tender. At the top of the boulder that crowned the rise of stones and thistles, Mary Agatha soon joined her. The hard stone surface was pocked where they stood, as if a thousand years of rain and wind had left their mark. The panorama below them stretched into the eternities as well. The desert shimmered, the glinting sand an ocean of copper and gold. Beyond the barren valley, rocky buttes rose in random piles, and farther on, pewter mountains lined the horizon like a ragged frame against the sky. The sun was high, and Ruth scanned the scene beneath it, searching for any sign of movement—men on horseback, dust clouds signaling riders in the distance. She saw nothing until Mary Agatha pointed out a lone figure ranging along the foothills directly below them, then another, and two more.

"Them's our menfolk," she said abruptly. "Looks like they's still on the prowl. Our home place's the other way."

Ruth was both relieved and disappointed. Where were *her* menfolk, she wondered. Surely, a party of priesthood brethren was searching for her and Lucie. She wiped her brow with her sleeve and steadied herself on Mary Agatha's arm. The vista took her breath away, as Western horizons always did, and, with no sight of her rescuers, she said a silent prayer and focused on the beauty that was hers, a fresh reminder that God was near and had not forgotten them. The breeze ruffled through her hair, and she recognized its touch as something reassuring.

Mary Agatha was less enthusiastic. "This is a dry, forsaken country," she murmured, squinting at the scene. "Nature's left little blessing here."

"What about your plants? You said yourself they're nature's gift." Ruth nodded at the thistles the woman held. "Some blessings lie in secret until we recognize their worth."

Mary Agatha looked quizzically at Ruth, taken with her words. She set her collection of petals and foliage down and slipped to her haunches, still eyeing Ruth as she twisted to find some semblance of comfort. "You say ya tramped across this country once? You say ya come from where it's green and ya found this barren place? *This* was yer promised land?" The woman swept her arm across the vista, seeing only desolation, and looked at Ruth dubiously.

"God brought my people here, Mary Agatha."

"We wuz searchin' for God when we come too, I guess," said the woman. "All we found wuz weeds and rattlesnakes. Seems like God coulda chose a better place."

"A place is what you make of it," Ruth pressed, staring again at the distant peaks. "My Zion is surrounded by mountains, and with God's help we made it what it is. And its promise fulfills an ancient prophecy in the Bible. '*And it shall come to pass in the last days, that the mountain of the Lord's house shall be established in the top of the mountains, and shall be exalted above the hills; and all nations shall flow unto it. And many people shall go and say, Come ye, and let us go up to the mountain of the Lord, to the house of the God of Jacob; and he will teach us of his ways, and we will walk in his paths: for out of Zion shall go forth the law, and the word of the Lord from Jerusalem.*' That's where Lucie and I live, Mary Agatha, in the Lord's Zion, in the tops of mountains like these. You're right. When I first came to Zion as a young girl, I saw only the harshness of it. Now, as a mature woman, I recognize its beauty and its symbol. Just as your weeds produce syrups that heal, a rugged land can produce strong people." Ruth paused and silently scanned the landscape once again. When she turned, Mary Agatha was still staring, caught in the spell of Ruth's words. "I love *these* mountains too," Ruth added. "They're symbols of strength just as mine at home are. Perhaps *your* strength, Mary Agatha."

Mary Agatha shrugged self-consciously. Ruth watched her as the breeze ruffled the strands of gray hair around her face.

"Someday, I'm going to write a poem about the strength and firmness of mountains," Ruth continued, "and how we can stand as stalwart as they do."

"I like the notion of that," said Mary Agatha. She was still staring intently at Ruth, hanging on her last word, anticipating the next. "You know, I ain't never had no woman friend," she blurted suddenly. "No woman to talk to, anyways."

"You have one now." Ruth smiled. Mary Agatha was letting her guard down, Ruth knew, and she reacted with gentleness.

The strange woman turned to scan the horizon again, that velvet rim of blue sky settled against the mountains on the east. "There's something holy about you," she said, looking back at Ruth. "You ain't like the others. You see beauty where they see wind and waste. You use pretty words, while theirs is bitter. You read those hard lines in that Book of Mormon and make 'em sound like music, even when I can't keep up with ever'thing they mean. There's power in your gentleness, Sister Ruth, that I cain't quite track. I cain't put my finger on it except to say it's holy and beyond my notion of this world."

"You overrate me, dear Mary," responded Ruth, embarrassed by the praise.

But the woman would not be silenced. She eyed Ruth with a strange intent that was almost stern, and her lips were oddly quivering as she spoke. "You walked through the sand of a desert behind Ez Brackett to save a girl who ain't yer own when there's no way you can save her by yerself. Ya got no gun, no muscle. All ya can do is be here with her, an' here ya are. Here with some gentle power that I cain't track. Yer like my wildflowers, Ruth. They hold a secret—a healin' secret, like you said—that no one knows until someone studies up on 'em. Then the mystery is uncovered. I ain't quite tracked yer magic yet, but I know it's there, just like you see somethin' special in yer mountains, and I aim to ponder on that magic as long as we're together."

"You must know, Mary, that the source of any 'magic' I may have comes from my faith in Jesus Christ." Ruth looked out over the spacious scene again. "*How beautiful upon the mountains,*" she murmured, "*are the feet of him that bringeth good tidings; that publisheth peace.*"

"Say them words again," pleaded Mary. "I ain't never heard anything quite like that." Ruth repeated the lines and promised to show Mary where in the scriptures they were found. Mary's face was alight with wonder as she listened to Ruth's voice. The moment was fleeting. Soon the woman bent to her work again, and practical matters absorbed her attention as she bundled her harvest of weeds and wildflowers.

On the way back down the trail, Ruth was caught by a wave of disappointment and despair. She knew the scratches on the cider barrel board added up to eight already. She had desperately hoped to see some sign of the rescue party from her high vantage point today and instead found nothing. But only for a moment did Ruth waver. Only briefly did she lose her bearings. She did have the "magic" Mary Agatha saw. She did know its source as she had proclaimed. Remembering the poetic passage, she repeated it. "*How beautiful upon the mountains are the feet of him that bringeth good tidings . . .*" Soon the trail was firm again, its markings clear, and Ruth caught her breath and pressed forward, energized by her own determined faith. Mary Agatha was right. Ruth had a special gift, but it was not magic nor mysterious. It was as real as the natural wilderness around her. She had the Holy Ghost and other gifts of the Spirit bestowed upon her in her calling. That Mary Agatha should recognize those gifts without understanding their source was comforting to Ruth, though she took no credit for them. Her faith was strengthened. God was with her. Israel's army was not yet in sight, but its Captain stood beside her with His consoling hand.

***

That night in the cabin, after Ez Brackett and the other men had arrived home, leaving Ruth tense and apprehensive, she turned again to prayer. Lucie was asleep, Mary Agatha was finishing the outside chores, and Ruth was left alone to ponder the gravity of her situation and plead with the Lord for sustenance. She and Lucie had lived another day without rescue, and there was apparently none in sight. What should they do? Where could they turn? As if in answer, Ruth felt a new warmth envelope her soul, a heavenly assurance that filled her with confidence and power, and she knew that even if an earthly rescue never came, she and Lucie would be all right.

Brackett made a visit to the cabin late that night, bending over Lucie like a crook-billed vulture ready to pounce. Ruth was still on fire. Staying near the bed and staring Brackett down with her piercing eyes, she tried to make herself larger than she was, a constant obstacle to the man in his efforts to get close to the girl. He always looked at Lucie so leeringly, and Ruth hated every gesture. "I have a hankerin' to see her tonight," he told Ruth when she tried to get in his way.

"She's asleep," Ruth whispered with hiss and tenacity, "and don't you wake her with your noisy boots."

But it was too late. Lucie opened her eyes, and Ruth saw them widen in fear. She slipped closer to the girl, arm outstretched as if to fend off an intruder. It was a useless gesture, she knew, but the body language was unmistakable.

Brackett usually found it easy to ignore Ruth—all one hundred pounds of her—bull his way into the cabin, and with his bulk and growl suppress any opposition. But Ruth's fire tonight subdued him. He looked about the little room as if he were a stranger there, and it was several minutes before he licked his bulbous lips and remarked sullenly, "The women say you've had her up and walkin' round. She's better off than you been tellin' me."

At this remark, Lucie came to life and struggled backward toward the wall, terrified.

"'Walking' is a poor description," Ruth shot back firmly, keeping herself within easy reach of the girl. "Her leg is badly broken and needs to remain immovable to heal properly. We've helped her up so she can keep good muscle tone and circulation, but we've kept the leg protected. That, Mr. Brackett, will be required for a good long time."

"She can stay down in bed forever," Brackett snorted darkly in reply, "but pretty soon I aim to join her there and take my place as her new husband. It's what she needs, a man to make her feel alive again." He sneered and rubbed his black whiskers as he noted Ruth's repulsion. "Don't worry, Sister Ruth. I won't be messin' with her broken leg."

"You're no husband to her," declared Ruth, "and never will be."

In her corner, Lucie stared in horror, her back against the wall.

Brackett only laughed, an ugly, smarmy chortle. But there was hesitation now, and for a while he was silent and ponderous before he gathered enough of his wits to make slow conversation. He sank into the chair, letting Ruth stand by the bed and Lucie look on in trembling silence. "I don't know how yer gonna stop this marriage," he muttered testily to Ruth. "You ain't got no stake in Lucie's life or mine, and you'd be a fool to think ya did. I've been patient with ya, even accommodatin'. I'm lettin' ya stay in this cabin. I'm givin' ya food and shelter, and I ain't bothered ya none. I've let you and Mary Agatha tend to Lucie as ya please when I coulda left ya in the desert, hog-tied to a cedar tree till someone run across ya. It'd a been a lot less trouble than puttin' up with things now and not knowin' what to do with ya when it's over."

"What *will* you do with me, Mr. Brackett, when it's *over*? Have you ever thought of that?" Ruth raised an eyebrow, feeling fearless and in control.

Brackett squirmed a little. "I don't know yet," he finally conceded. "Maybe I kin still find that cedar tree." Then, gaining his resolve, the man looked at Ruth scornfully, as if her courage angered him. He shot a salacious glance at Lucie before turning back to meet his nemesis. "Know this, Sister Ruth," he growled. "God gave me that girl there. He directed me where to find her. Ol' Jake Royal was a preacher back in the day. He'll say some words over us if it'll make ya feel any better, but Lucie belongs to me, and someday real soon I'm comin' here to take what's mine!"

***

After he had gone, Ruth spent half an hour calming Lucie, regretting that the girl had heard Brackett's direct and vicious threats. Later, she sat in the shadows, just watching Lucie sleep. She hoped Lucie truly meant what she finally told her in the end. "He'll never own me, Sister Fox, not with some trumped-up marriage. He'll never own my soul." Ruth looked at Lucie now and hoped she was dreaming of her real wedding day and of Albert strolling with her down a Salt Lake City avenue. She prayed that Lucie would continue to be strong. She prayed for her own endurance as well.

Later, when Mary Agatha came into the cabin for the nightly scripture reading, Ruth never mentioned Brackett or his ugly words. Instead, she showed Mary Agatha where the verse about the mountains was found.

"I've never met no one like you," murmured Mary, taken by the verses. Her round eyes were still glowing as she looked at Ruth. "Lord knows, I never have."

Chapter Eleven
TOM LEAVITT'S GHOST

THERE WAS A REASON RUTH couldn't see a rescue party from her vantage point above the valley. Elder Burton's muster of riders was scouring the back side of a range of jagged cliffs just to the north. Having taken the wedge trail as Burton directed, they finally found their way through a box canyon that looked promising as a refuge for the spirit chasers. But in the end, it produced only dry sage and rocky ledges and no sign of a recent camp or village. Once out of the canyon, the men followed another narrow path and decided to head south again, exploring the foothills on the opposite side, clefts and ridges that were hidden from ready access. They spent another day combing the back side of a series of low, humpback mountains invisible from the valley side.

When the trail along the bottom of the ragged cliffs yielded nothing of interest after two more days of searching, some of the men left their horses staked in the scant prairie grasses and moved on foot, climbing a high butte in search of a broader perspective. Two of the climbers, linked together by a rope, lost their footing on loose rock chips, the one causing the other to slide back into him, leaving both with sprains, bruises, and lacerations. Dr. Morgan treated the wounds, but it had taken most of the morning, and it wasn't until late afternoon that anyone reached the high point of the bluff. Ray Sherman, the Church detective, knelt in the brush with his field glasses and scanned the desert below, while Washington County Sheriff Booker looked backward, squinting into the western sun.

It was Sherman who first saw the lone figure moving slowly across the broad plain on a horse. The detective steadied himself and held the glasses tighter. Was it really a rider so small in the distance, that tiny blot against the landscape? Was it a shadow or a ghost? Sherman nudged Patch Booker and handed him the glasses, pointing in the direction of the blot, and soon the sheriff nodded. Slipping down flat on his belly and steadying his elbows for another look, he liked what he saw. "The fellow's alone, all right," he said. "I don't see a wagon or no one else around. We got most of the local fellows with us, so this stranger is someone to check out. If he *ain't* a spirit chaser, maybe he's seen something."

At the bottom of the butte, Sherman reported the sighting to Jennings Burton, who immediately ordered most of the men to mount up. Leaving Dr. Morgan with instructions to follow once the injured climbers could travel, Burton began the long trail with the others, through the wedge between the cliffs to the valley. There, the road from Modena to St. George provided some sense of direction. The traveler was the only sign of anyone for miles. Most of the men, valiant in their faith but weary from their search, were both eager and apprehensive about who he was and what he could tell them. Some had begun to despair for Ruth May Fox and her young companion, and they hated the idea that they had failed.

***

The dark figure that Burton and his troop were approaching was Cal Brackett, and the story of how he ended up alone and away from camp to be spotted by the rescuers was a likely one, given his temperament. But it would have stunned Ruth had she known it. She had believed that her and Lucie's fate depended primarily on her own strength and determination, her ability to hang on until help arrived. She hadn't counted on a petty quarrel leading to a possible rescue. But sometimes evil collapses on itself, being anchored on the sifting sands of hatred, envy, and division.

Cal Brackett had been spoiling for a fight ever since Ez brought Ruth and Lucie into camp. Even the ten-day wager, made in a moment of drunken hubris, eventually diminished in importance. Cal lost interest in it when his own winning number passed on the fourth day, but he continued to brood over the danger Ruth and Lucie presented. From then on, he groused and fumed and snorted, spitting out his objections to anyone who would listen. "Ez is bringing trouble on us," he growled to Jacob Royal and the Grovers. "Why didn't he jus' take that freighter's goods and let the women be? No one would look very long for a bunch of tools and dishes, but no one will *stop* lookin' for these women. We was safe cuz no one cared. Now they will, and Ez done that to us. He took away the one good thing we had."

The day the men rode along the draws and foothills ostensibly looking for the strays, Cal was wound tighter than usual. The storm and the subsequent hard work it necessitated had irritated him. He blamed Ruth and Lucie for taking up the cabin, when he and his wife could have been better sheltered from the rain. The muddy puddles of the camp soaked his old boots, warping them out of shape. The wasted camp clutter swimming in the ditches reminded him of the sty he lived in, and he felt cheated by Ez's personal priorities. Most of all, he was jealous of Ezra's control, jealous of the pretty girl Ez brought home to marry, jealous of his brother's domination. The envy ate at him. It was a notion that he scratched like an old scab until it bled.

On the trail, Cal was sullen and obdurate. Finding that one of his dogs had put his nose in a skunk hole didn't improve his attitude, and as the men lounged under the scant shade of the pinion trees and ate their lunch of coarse bread and jerky, a flask of liquor was produced, and drinking always brought out the worst in the younger Brackett. Soon he was complaining bitterly.

"There was useful goods on that freight wagon," he began. "Saws, I'll bet, and maybe a chisel or two. That freighter's known to have good tools." Cal eyed his brother petulantly. "I didn't see ya bring nuthin' like that home." Cal gestured with his flask. When the other men ignored him and Ez only chuckled, Cal grew increasingly testy.

"There was blankets in the freight wagon too. And I'm sleepin' on a corn-husk mattress with no good cover. And I know that fellow who drives the freight woulda had plenty we could use. That wagon's been around here ten years at least. I've seen it loaded to the spokes with all sorts of plunder. I'll bet that fella was carryin' a nice Henry rifle I coulda used, and it's likely there was a Colt's revolver in his belt."

"Warn't no Colt's revolver," growled Ez.

"The Henry, then. The freighter musta had a Henry."

"I don't know what he had. I didn't care."

"No, ya didn't," spat Cal, rising to confront his brother. "All ya cared for was yer own wants, Ez, and ya brung that girl to camp, and it's gonna mean an end to us once the law comes prowlin'. They wouldn't give a devil about an old Henry and some blankets, but they'll be crawling down our throats over this girl and the woman with her."

"I ain't seen no lawmen yet," said Ezra, chewing on his jerky.

"You will. You'll see 'em. And we'll all be made to pay." Cal turned to the other men, trying to press his point. "You fellas should be scared as well, lettin' Ez here put ya in harm's way. He coulda helped y'all if he'd a let those women be and stole the freight instead. Why, the freighter himself wouldn't a bothered with a little thievery if his passengers was safe. I'll bet on that."

"I don't know, Cal," mused Grover, who had spent some time in St. George. "Tom Leavitt worried a bunch about his freight."

"You knew the freighter, Joe? I didn't know ya knew 'im." It was Cal who spoke.

Joe Grover shot a glance at Ez and answered casually. "Name's Leavitt, I think. Tom Leavitt. Been freightin' a long time. I didn't really *know* 'im, and he sure don't know me. I jus' heard the name, that's all, and how he took his job serious when it come to what he hauled. Seems he had to get a bigger wagon from the one he used to drive, folks trusted him with so much freight. It's what I heard anyways."

Cal grew impatient with Grover. He paced back and forth as he listened to Grover's opinion about Leavitt, but soon Cal turned away. His fight was with his brother, and he got in Ez's face to make his point. "Well, I say this here Leavitt wouldn't risk a dustup over a few blankets, and next time I see ol' Tom, I'm gonna up and ask 'im."

"You ain't gonna do that," said Ez dully.

"Sure I am. Just watch me."

"The freight driver's dead, Cal. You ain't askin' him nuthin'."

Cal's mouth dropped open. He stood rigid, stunned by this new fact. Then his face soured. Leavitt was no friend, only a passing figure on the trail, but murder added to the burdens Ez had piled on them, and Cal exploded at the news. "What d' ya mean, the freighter's dead? Ya never tol' me ya killed 'im. Ya never tol' me that!"

"It was an accident. When the carriage rolled and the girl busted her leg, the freighter hit his head and died. I warn't no cause of it. I didn't kill 'im."

Cal lunged forward, grabbed Ez by the shirt, and tried to pull him to his feet. He was drunk and wild now and filled with rage. "Ya've killed *us*! Ya've killed all of us! We coulda let the women go and faded into the wild like we always done, but the law won't let that happen now. We're done for, Ez! Ya've killed us!"

Ez was on his feet. He jerked away from his brother's grip and slapped him soundly with the back of his hand. Cal stumbled backward, smarting at the blow. Outraged, he lunged forward, swinging his fists and flailing both arms as he tried to strike out at his brother. Ez dodged about and finally threw himself at Cal straight on. Soon both men were rolling in the dirt, kicking and scratching and growling like animals. Their companions formed a silent circle around them, tense and anxious but reluctant to interfere. Nor did they cheer for one brother or the other. They were forced to live with both men and wished to make no enemies. The brothers tangled and rolled and punched each other. At one point, Ez drove Cal's head into the ground, and it thudded against the sand like a melon dropped from a produce wagon. The younger man was scrappy and fought hard, but Ez was the bigger brute, and in a few minutes his weight got the better of feisty Cal, who was kicked and pounded unmercifully until he lay bleeding and groaning in a rumpled heap at his brother's feet.

"The freighter's dead!" Ez shouted in panting spurts as Cal lay writhing in the dirt in front of him. "He's still lying down there by his wrecked wagon for all I know. Sure, I left his plunder, his pots and pans and blankets. But I brung home somethin' better, an' I aim to marry her. Ya got no say about it, Cal. We'll fade into the mountains like we always done, first sight of any lawman. They ain't a-gonna stop me or take Lucie from me—and neither are you."

He turned and trudged away as Jacob Royal and another man brought water to young Cal and began pressing a damp rag to his bloody face.

When Cal Brackett finally came around and was able to sit up again, he was in no mood to remain with his brother and the other men as they made their way back home. His wounds were smarting; his body ached. There was a violent thumping in his head. Sullenly, he refused any proffer of aid except water, and he kept to himself, folded up in a bushy corner as the others tended to the stock and prepared to leave. Lingering until the sun dipped behind the mountain, they took their time, lazily pondering in any shade they could find. The fight had dampened their spirits for further horseplay. Ez was silent and morose, determined to let Cal sulk, believing he would lick his wounds and come to life again once the troop moved toward home. But the shouts of the men and the stirring of the horses drove the defeated Cal inside himself, and he did nothing more to help.

Instead, he sat alone with glazed eyes and little interest. The others mounted finally and rode by him silently. When Ez passed, he paused to look down from his saddle at his brother. The big black gelding under him was frisky and anxious to follow the other riders on the path. Ez had two strays he was leading and little time to talk. Like Cal, he was smarting from the fight, although his wounds were far less serious. "We're takin' off, then," he said, expecting some vile gesture in return. When Cal did not immediately respond, Ez swung his reins and moved away, sullen and unconcerned.

"I'm gonna go get that plunder," Cal suddenly cried. "Maybe I kin find that Henry rifle and take 'er off ol' Leavitt."

"Yer a fool," bellowed Ez over his shoulder. "Most likely, the law's found Leavitt by now and all his freight. Ya go messin' around over there, they're gonna think you done it."

"If we're gonna have to pay for this war, we might as well get the spoils," whined Cal. "Ya got yers. I'm goin' after mine."

"Suit yerself," shouted Ez finally. With one more nod at his brother, he wheeled the horses around to find the narrow trail through the sagebrush. He expected Cal to catch up shortly, once he'd nursed his pride awhile. That he never appeared was only a curiosity that night. Ez had other things on his mind.

What Cal Brackett did *was* foolish. But greed and curiosity ruled him. Greed and the ache to somehow better his brother—or at least equal him. And since the law was bound to seek them out eventually, even the risk of his own arrest paled against his need for spite. "I'll nose around and get what I can from the freight, and I'll find ol' Leavitt too. Likely, he had money on 'im." Hate and anger and a fuzzy brain drove Cal Brackett. "Ez won't keep that girl for long with the law a-huntin' for us. But I'll maybe git some plunder while their backs are turned and end up a winner after all, able to thumb my nose at Ez for what he done to me."

With such notions rushing through his skull, Cal turned his horse toward the broad prairie on the east, leaving the foothills behind. It was several miles to the Modena road, and he likely passed over the same sand and brush the travois had coursed through just ten days before. He'd waited until the sun was low with enough time before dusk to take advantage of the cooler hours and the light. Even in the rising shadows, he moved on, guided by the moon and the line of distant mountains he knew. Before the sky turned black, he'd found the road, a ribbon in the starlight that would lead him straight to his destination in the morning.

Cold now, the desert still protected him. He found a soft bed in the sand and pulled some leaves and branches from a brittle bush for a pillow, wrapping his poncho over his shoulders and under his head. His wounds from the fight with Ez still pained him. His head still ached. But the morning promised something he could prize.

***

The men from St. George had not left Tom Leavitt's body behind. Under Patch Booker's orders, two of them had escorted their supply wagon back to town with Leavitt respectfully aboard, and the freight driver now lay in a coffin at the local funeral parlor, waiting for his only brother to arrive from Arizona. There was nothing human left in the gully, dead or alive. Only the carriage wreckage remained, still floating in the puddles left by the storm, and Cal Brackett had no trouble finding it just off the road and upside down in the muddy wash.

After stirring about and searching in vain for Leavitt's body, Cal gleefully explored the site, turning over every piece of litter, breaking open every case and trunk. Rawhide, blankets, the tools bound for Salt Lake, even Fenton Meade's discarded coat excited him, although most everything was wet and muddy, ruined by the storm. Cal Brackett was a looter and saw only treasure in his path. The broken wood from the wagon could kindle his fire. The cushions from the seats could pillow his head. He stripped them all, leaving nothing he could use. Then he found a stick and dug a hole in the side of the gully, where he piled everything he couldn't carry. He covered the place with brush and weeds, preserving his treasure until he could return. He lamented the fact that he found no gun, no Henry rifle or Colt's revolver. But he smiled at what he did have, what he had reaped from his excursion. "Hah!" he muttered to himself, "Ez is gonna thank me for savin' what he left behind."

But all the while Cal lingered over his find, for all the satisfaction he enjoyed, a dull, oppressive spirit possessed him too. "It's the freighter," he told himself warily. "His ghost is hoverin' here. He's angry about the stuff all broken, the dishes and the tools, but most of all he's angry about the women Ez took. On this road they belonged to him." The man began to stagger under this burden that played relentlessly with his mind. The headache that lingered became the punishment Tom Leavitt's spirit was exacting. Cal searched for peace and relief in the shade of the awning where Lucie had been. Its remains still hung sadly on one side, and he pulled it over his face when the sun was high. Later, he roamed to the end of the gully and back, still finding no remedy for his depression. Then he recognized

Ez Brackett's red bandana, still tied to the marking post, ruffled by the breeze, and the color of it hurt his eyes. "Blood," he murmured to himself. "Ez killed a man. He shed a man's blood so he could steal from him, and the fella's still here, angry about what Ez done."

In the end, Cal left almost everything behind. Tom Leavitt's ghost wouldn't stop tormenting him. The gray fog in his mind wouldn't lift. The sun was still high and hot when he finally began moving listlessly back from where he'd come, unconcerned about the searing temperature. A drum in his head was pounding—Tom Leavitt beating on a tom-tom, driving him away.

At first, he muttered promises to himself about all the loot he would soon come back to retrieve once the freighter's spirit had flown away and the place was silent again. "I hid it good," he told himself, unmindful of the tools that were dropping from his poorly packed saddlebags and the blankets he had wrapped the goods in. After a few miles, his purpose for being where he was had disappeared altogether, and he looked back in confused wonder at what was discarded on the trail.

Late in the day when Jennings Burton and the men found him, Cal Brackett was delirious, not begging for water but crying about some demon that was following him and wouldn't let him rest. When Burton asked him about Ruth Fox and Lucie Cole, he was more than willing to tell what he knew. "Ez took 'em," he said. "And none of us will get no peace till they're free. Leavitt's seen to that. I'll take ya to 'em soon as I can walk."

"I think this man has recently suffered a severe blow to the head," James Colvin whispered, "and the heat has nearly driven him mad. Can we trust what he's tellin' us?"

"Yes, I think we can," answered Burton. "He's too far gone to lie."

Chapter Twelve
THE EDGE OF ETERNITY

ONCE HER LATEST CONFRONTATION WITH Ez Brackett had ended, Ruth spent several restless hours trying to draw strength from her many gifts—reason, spiritual insight, faith—as she searched the scriptures diligently. "*Whosoever shall put their trust in God shall be supported in their trials,*" she read in Alma, "*and their troubles, and their afflictions, and shall be lifted up at the last day.*" Then in Jacob, "*You that are pure in heart . . . Look unto God with firmness of mind, and pray unto him with exceeding faith, and he will console you in your afflictions, and he will plead your cause, and send down justice upon those who seek your destruction.*"

Ruth pondered these passages and prayed for understanding. That the words sustained her, there was no doubt. But did they imply a spiritual resolution or a mortal one? Was the ultimate promise meant to be fulfilled in the eternities rather than on a dry, desolate plain near Modena, Utah, in 1903? Was the Lord's consoling hand only for the future, when the wicked were finally judged and the righteous redeemed and relieved of their burdens?

She remembered praying for her baby Eliza so many years before. How she had pleaded so earnestly for her child to recover. The Lord did indeed bless her with peace when Eliza died and with the assurance that Ruth would see her again in the afterlife. Was that the message here? All would be well in the eternities but not necessarily now?

Ruth had known many worthy souls who had pleaded for blessings in their prayers and still experienced great sorrow. She believed with all her heart in divine promises, but were they meant for a different time? Human beings had no perspective. The scripture counseled her to "look unto God with a firmness of mind," meaning, she supposed, that He expected her to use her intelligence and intuition. Perhaps she should do anything she could to save Lucie's life rather than worry so much about the "marriage" Brackett had in mind. Maybe she should walk away, go for help, brave the wild at first light. If she stole a horse, she'd be followed. But if she merely walked away, no one would care. Perhaps she shouldn't wait for daylight. She could sneak through the slot canyon with a lantern. She knew it well enough by now. Modena couldn't be too far. Twenty miles at the most.

Certainly, they would all be gone when she got back with a posse—Ez and Mary Agatha, Gertie and Clara, Jacob Royal and the Grovers, and of course Lucie. They would slip away as they'd always done before, fading into the wilderness like shadows. But sooner or later they would be found. Ruth knew them. She could give the authorities the clues they needed. She could point them in the right direction. She could help them eventually bring Lucie home—not unscathed, perhaps, but alive and ready to resume her plans, her happy life, her destiny with Albert Covington.

There in the candlelight, watching Lucie sleep, Ruth pondered this option with great intensity. Was this what she should do? In the end, she decided against it. There were practical considerations, to be sure. Twenty miles was a long way in the desert for a woman traveling alone on foot. And if she failed for any reason, Lucie would be lost.

But finally her decision rested on one thing. *I will not leave this girl alone. I am her only connection to everything that's pure and holy— not me precisely, for I'm only a flawed mortal. But in my calling and in this situation, I represent her tether to the Lord. If I must die to save her or watch her suffer for the sins of others, I'll hold her hand. I will not break that bond.*

That night when Mary Agatha came to help with Lucie's needs and to putter with her dishes and bottles, Ruth asked her again about the Henry rifle. "Are you sure you haven't seen it anywhere? Does Cal Brackett have it? Jacob Royal? Someone must know where it is."

"Anyone had a gun like that, I'd see it," said Mary Agatha. She was crushing the leaves and stems from their recent hike and showed little interest in Ruth's questions. Lucie, however, listened closely from where she sat against her pillow. Her body was healing. She was in less pain and becoming more involved in the urgency of the moment. The latest threat from Brackett had stunned and shaken her. While she'd become stronger through the crisis—emotionally as well as physically—she still experienced bouts of panic and depression. Sometimes she would shiver uncontrollably for no obvious reason, trying to hold back tears that finally ran down her cheeks as she lay quietly watching Ruth read or Mary putter at the table. Sometimes a solemn silence engulfed the girl for hours as she watched the others work.

Alert to every sign of doubt in Lucie, Ruth continually sought ways to counter her anxiety. Tonight she'd cheerily fussed with the girl's appearance. They'd had no hairbrush, but with the lather of a yucca root, she'd washed Lucie's hair and dried it with her petticoat, leaving the dark tresses glossy and beautiful. Seeing the girl so fresh and natural, even Mary Agatha had to smile. "It's a wonder how a good scrub can perk up folks in pain," she said, drawing an appreciative glance from Lucie.

Mary's compliment emboldened Ruth, who still had the Henry rifle on her mind. "How do you see this all ending, Mary Agatha, if Lucie and I can't defend ourselves?" Ruth said abruptly. "Surely you care about us. You care about what happens."

Mary Agatha continued to look at Lucie, but her eyes narrowed. "It'll end how it ends, Sister Ruth. What comes, comes. There's not much we mortals can do about it."

"But don't you care? Don't you care what happens to Lucie?" Ruth usually avoided speaking directly of Lucie's danger in front of the girl, but Mary Agatha's seeming indifference left Ruth desperate and frustrated. "Doesn't it bother you that she might be forced to . . . to marry a stranger who has brutally taken her from her family?"

The old woman turned to Ruth and considered the question pensively. Behind them, Lucie shifted nervously on the bed, her eyes wide and riveted on both of them. "God speaks to you, Sister Ruth,"

Mary Agatha finally whispered. "I know He does. Why else would ya care so much for a girl who ain't yer own? Why else would ya stay? No one's keepin' ya. Ya didn't have to come, an' ya could leave. It'd be a long walk, but ya could do it. Yet here ya stay."

"I stay for Lucie. She has no one else."

"And that's the thing I'm sayin'. Yer God's angel, Ruth. Ya got somethin' I don't have and cain't quite figure out." The woman shrugged and turned back to her roots and leaves. "Lucie there ain't no kin of mine. She got a busted leg, an' it interests me to try an' fix it. It interests me to hear ya read at night when everythin' is quiet. I like the sound of the words, and I like ponderin' their meanin'. But I got no special feelin' for anyone who ain't my kin—and only a little of that. God ain't spoke to me as He has to you. I got no truck with Him. But you, Ruth, yer somethin' different. God will tell ya what to do about Lucie, if it comes to that."

Ruth slipped down in the chair and smiled gently. This unenlightened woman had more faith than Ruth did. "God will help me," she finally told Mary Agatha wryly, "but I could still use that rifle."

Mary Agatha studied Ruth a moment. "I tol' ya I ain't seen no rifle," she said at last. "I'll keep my eyes open for it, but if it ain't loaded, like you said, I don't see what good it can do. An' it may be a gun does *more* harm sometimes." Mary Agatha probably had seen enough bullet wounds to know.

Later, alone in the cabin with Lucie, Ruth found one of Mary's silver pots that could adequately mirror Lucie's reflection, and she showed the girl her newly scrubbed face and hair. Lucie managed a grateful smile but set the pot aside without much primping. She took little joy in seeing the sadness the pot reflected. Ruth looked forlornly at the girl. She remembered her youthful excitement of only days ago, her animation and anticipation. All that had been erased by terror and pain. As her circumstances had changed, so had Lucie, of course. She seemed older and ready to think more seriously about taking a risk.

"If I could make it up on a horse," she said evenly, "we could ride away, Sister Fox. I'm well enough now that I'd be willing to try."

Ruth looked at Lucie's leg lying straight and firm, bound tightly with strips of rawhide and braced with the iron pokers. "I don't think that's possible," she answered softly, patting the trussed up leg, which was as heavy and stiff as a winter fire log.

"I've done quite a bit of riding," Lucie pressed. "We have horses at home. My father and my brothers take me along sometimes on their hunting trips. I think I could manage to stay mounted. If someone could help me up, I'm sure I could hang on."

Ruth knew that Lucie was grasping at any thread of hope. But even if she were somehow able to mount a horse in her condition, the narrow slot canyon would prove impassable. "You're a brave girl, Lucie," she finally said, "but we're going to have to find another way."

***

Rays of sun coming through the brittle chinks of the cabin awakened them in the morning and filled the room with a mottled sepia glow, a warm old-fashioned tinge that somehow whispered elegance. Ruth began the morning as she always did, checking first on Lucie. Her freshly washed, thick hair lay fuzzy and shapeless against the pillow, for they'd had no way to curl or comb it. Ruth smiled, noticing again how beautiful Lucie was in spite of her ungroomed look. *Heaven knows, that's how all young woman are*, Ruth thought—so lovely in their mortal prime, so vulnerable both in body and in spirit.

Waking, Lucie saw Ruth's benevolent smile and seemed to read her thoughts. "I'm a sight, I'll bet," she said, mustering a giggle.

"You are," Ruth answered. "A lovely one."

There was another pause as each of them contemplated the day that lay ahead. *The tenth day of the wager*, Ruth remembered. Lucie took a deep breath and let her wide eyes rove the little room. After a moment, she whispered gently, "I want you to know, Sister Fox, that I won't lose my faith over this, whatever happens. I laid awake last night thinking about everything. Our ancestors suffered far worse, and they still kept striving. Remember what you said about them in that last speech you gave? Something about carrying on no matter what. Bad things happen, but we carry on. I owe it to them—and to you—not to weaken in the face of adversity."

Ruth put a loving arm around the girl's shoulders and hugged her close. "Ah, Lucie," she said cheerfully, "we're going to make it through this, you and I."

***

That evening Ruth decided to confront Ezra Brackett, away from the cabin and before he came for his nightly ogling of Lucie. Ruth had had enough of that, and she was determined to try again to reason with the man, to remind him once more of the risk he was taking, the destruction he was bringing to his entire community by committing so terrible a crime.

She found him watering the tethered horses at the back of the camp and approached with all the courage she could muster. Watching him for a moment before he noticed her, Ruth was struck with the irony of the scene. Brackett was brushing each pony with a coarse-toothed comb; wetting the animal's hide down; cleaning the mud away; and working to smooth each ragged place where stones, fence posts, and thistles had left their mark. He combed each horse's tangled mane, slapped away the flies, and examined each hoof carefully. Ruth had heard of men who treated their animals better than their women. Now here was proof, and it was a bitter thing to see.

Ruth let him become aware of her and watched as he continued his work without comment.

"I don't want you coming to the hut tonight," she finally began stoutly. "You frighten Lucie, and she needs her rest."

"Seems like all she does is rest," said Brackett without looking up. "Someday she'll have to earn her place around here—and so will you."

"Mr. Brackett, do you honestly feel that's going to happen? Do you really think that Lucie's ever going to stay with you of her own free will?"

Brackett considered this, thoughtfully rubbing his beard. "Maybe not at first, but once we're man and wife and it's all been consummated, what else can she do? Eve was made to have desires toward her husband, and that's how it'll be once we're married. I've got no fears in that regard."

"Then fear this: the law is coming for you, Mr. Brackett. Your whole village here is going to be broken up, the women and children taken away. The law won't let you live like animals anymore." Suddenly, Ruth's fists were clenched, her eyes piercing. "Hear me, Mr. Brackett. Lucie isn't yours and never will be. Don't make things harder on yourself or your family by committing a crime to get something you can't have."

Brackett dropped his curry brush into the nearest bucket. He looked Ruth in the eye. "A crime is only in how it's thought of. It ain't a crime for us to scratch a livin' from what's put in our way. It ain't a crime for a man to take a wife that he's directed to find. It ain't a crime for us to live like we want, keepin' to ourselves an' makin' our own rules. Folks tryin' to mess with us, now that's a crime. It's all in how it's thought of, and my thinkin' don't match yours."

Ruth was exasperated. "Let us go," she pleaded. "Let me take Lucie in a wagon to Modena. I'll probably find our rescuers on the way. They can't be far. In the meantime, you and your people can fade into the wilderness, as you're always saying. We'll each go our own way."

"I cain't do that, Sister Ruth," said Brackett with finality. He picked up one of the buckets, slung his coat over his shoulder, and began walking away, shuffling and sputtering as he passed. Ruth followed him, still determined to coax, to beg, to plead. Finally, he abruptly stopped, put his bucket down, and turned to her.

"I cain't wait no longer to cozy up to Lucie. I cain't wait no longer to kiss and cozy up to her, prime her for her weddin' so to speak. My brother, Cal, took off in a huff yesterday. It's likely he'll run into yer posse down below somewhere. The fool'll lead 'em up here, sure as the devil. He's mad enough at me to do it just for spite, but if he don't, those men of yours will find a way to make him. I know we ain't got much time." Brackett snorted at his own stupidity. "I made a wager with Jacob Royal and the boys that I'd leave off Lucie for ten days. Well, the ten days has passed. But even if they hadn't,

Cal's spite's changed everything. We're gonna haff to leave here come tomorrow. There's no two ways about it." He paused and looked about the camp, seeming to consider all the work that faced him. Then he barked at Ruth with stubborn resolve. "Jacob's got some itch about marryin' me and Lucie proper, but I ain't got time for all that now." He paused and stooped to pick up the bucket again, rising with fierce determination in his eyes. "I want you and Mary Agatha to clear out of the cabin come first light. Don't be stirrin' around and in my way. I'm gonna be alone with Lucie in the morning. It might be that it's my only chance before we have to gather things up and get lost from yer people, and I ain't puttin' it off no longer. You hear me, Ruth? No longer."

With that, he walked away, and Ruth stood shivering in the rising shadows as darkness settled down on the cluttered camp.

Chapter Thirteen

CRUCIBLE

Ruth spent the rest of the night searching for a weapon. She rooted through the cabin, scattering Mary Agatha's tin dishes and bottles, and tried to sharpen the long end of a piece of kindling on a shard of glass to no avail. She revisited the lean-to where she had first awakened in this strange and dirty village and where she last remembered seeing Tom Leavitt's Henry rifle, but there was nothing useful to be found. In the dark of night, she edged quietly around the fire pits, their embers still aglow, fingering each of the crude utensils scattered there. The shabby, battered dog wakened from his hole, growled at her, and bared his teeth. When he recognized her scent, he wandered off. But she found nothing helpful anyway.

Brackett's pewter coffee mug hung in its place on the post near the table plank, if only to remind her of his reprehensible behavior toward the children, cuffing Luke Royal for hiding it. *"Ya touch my cup again, I'll box yer ear!"* she remembered Brackett shouting, sending the boy scurrying away in terror. Yes, she needed a strong weapon against a man who was capable of such abuse, and she was determined to find it. But would anything short of a rifle be enough?

The women used a long butcher knife when they cooked. She'd seen it. Where was that knife now? They had used an ax and a hatchet to cut the branches into kindling after the storm. What had become of those? But what good would any of these things do even if she found them? Brackett outweighed her by a hundred pounds and more. She'd be no match against him with a knife or hatchet. Still, she searched. There was something she could use. There had to be.

She thought of David and the five smooth stones he used against Goliath. Such a timid weapon, a slingshot, but it did the job. Of course, David had the armor of the Lord about him and the faith to face a giant. Ruth had faith but no sling and no smooth stones. In desperation she returned to the cabin, finding Lucie awake and waiting. "Anything?" asked Lucie apprehensively. And Ruth shook her head, dropping wearily into her chair, still trying to think of what to do.

"Our men will be here in the morning," said Lucie hopefully. "Brackett's right to worry. The rescuers have found his brother, and they will make him lead them here. They're only waiting till it's light."

Ruth nodded, buoyed by Lucie's faith, and suddenly she rose from the chair, an idea racing through her mind. Like Lucie, she believed that the rescue party would be there in the morning, but how soon? It dawned on her that delaying the enemy until help arrived might be as good as defeating him.

Turning around, Ruth scanned the row of tin cups, plates, and saucers that Mary Agatha had stacked against the wall. She searched intently for the fennel leaves and the butterfly weed, remembering the caution, *"Two strong gulps of this'll kill ya or light yer gut on fire. Add a little catnip to it, an' you'll sleep for hours—if yer lucky—and wake up rarin' to empty yer belly of anything it's got."* Mary Agatha had said this cheerily, as if she'd found triumph in something so simple as a laxative and a sleeping aid. *"That's why I like usin' 'em together. One of 'em puts ya to sleep while the other's doin' its work. Either way, yer gonna be down a spell, sicker than a hound dog in a snake pit. But if it don't kill ya, it'll heal ya, like a lot of things in this ol' world."*

Ruth found what she was looking for, the threadlike leaves of the fennel flower Mary Agatha had pointed out and the spear-shaped butterfly weed whose tea was toxic if made too strong. With Lucie's help, she crushed the leaves of both, added water, and let the mixture steep in a cup over the candle. Then she carefully repeated the process with Mary Agatha's precious catnip leaves, leaves whose tea promised restful sleep when ingested moderately. Ruth was not concerned with "restful" sleep or moderation. All she wanted was something that would incapacitate a two-hundred-fifty-pound man for several hours, and she hoped that either nausea or drowsiness would do it.

While Lucie watched with barely suppressed eagerness, Ruth labored over a midnight candle, painstakingly stirring the tea into a sticky, clear syrup. Her hands were agile, her fingers facile and well trained. Occasionally smiling at Lucie, she mixed the brew and impressed the girl again with her resourcefulness. "Mary Agatha says you're an angel, Sister Fox," murmured Lucie. "She means a real, earthbound angel who's unspotted from this world. She thinks you're the Lord's own courier to those less able. She thinks spiritual perfection is your special gift."

Ruth looked at Lucie, embarrassed by the praise. "Mary Agatha has tasted very little of the earth's goodness," she responded, still busy with the syrup. "The slightest kindness, the least bit of beauty or intellectual fire touches her like a torch. I'm as flawed as anyone and certainly more so than many. I'm no heavenly saint—though we both have that earthly title."

"Still . . ." said Lucie, hesitating, "when some urgent crisis comes my way again, I want you there with me. Then I'll have some hope that it will all turn out right." The girl's dark eyes were fixed on Ruth, who was too humbled to reply.

The syrup bubbled in the cup; the candle glowed. And Lucie would remember forever the amber light reflecting on her companion's lovely, sun-browned face.

Through the darkness, Ruth tiptoed down the path to the central fire pit and the nearby post where Brackett's favorite pewter cup hung on its upper twig. Nearby was the cider barrel board where ten scratches now appeared as evidence of the need for urgency even though the wager had taken second place to Cal Brackett's failure to come home.

Ruth wanted to kick the cider barrel. She wanted to break the board and its slashes into pieces. She hated everything it stood for, including the time that she and Lucie had wasted in this dirty, disheveled village. Studiously avoiding the barrel, she took the pewter cup and held it tightly in her fingers. Sometimes victories come by stealth instead of rage.

When Ruth returned to the cabin, it took her only seconds to rub the clear, sticky ointment she'd concocted around the inside of the entire mug. She worked carefully with her fingers, making sure that every part of the cup, from its bottom to its rim, was thoroughly coated. "It won't do that much harm," she told Lucie, "but let's hope it does enough."

"You're sure that he won't see or smell it first?"

"I don't think so. It's clear and sticky, and the coffee's strong and black and bitter. It should cover any other odor as soon as it's poured. It might dilute the catnip too much, but we'll hope for a stomachache at least. All we need is a little time. I'm sure our men are heading here at first light."

Satisfied that the cup was sufficiently covered with the paste, Ruth quietly retraced her steps down the path and hung the mug back on its high twig, taking a moment to listen for any sign that she might have been seen. Back in the cabin, she prayed again that Israel's army was close at hand and that Ezra Brackett would drink his coffee first thing in the morning.

Restless though she was, Ruth must have dozed, for she woke suddenly to gray shadows in the room and the chill of dawn. Pale light filtered through the slits of the walls, and she could hear the chirp of birds outside and the snorting of the horses down below. She sat up with a start and looked immediately at Lucie, who was still asleep. Remembering, she moved quickly to the door, opening it enough to scan the camp and spy the pewter cup still dangling from its twig. Clara Tophorn was stirring the embers at the fire pit, and even from the cabin, Ruth could see the charred old coffee pot steaming in its place among the coals.

Ruth dressed quickly and washed in the bucket Mary Agatha had left. Then she cleared away any remaining sign that she had tampered with the woman's herbs and potions. Her nerves on edge, Ruth kept a frequent vigil at the slit in the wall, watching for Ez Brackett to greet the sun and stumble toward his cup. His threats of yesterday echoed in her mind: "*I'm gonna be alone with Lucie in the morning. I'm gonna cozy up to her, prime her for her wedding, so to speak. It might be my only chance before we have to gather things and clear on out. I won't put it off no longer!*" Surely, some reckoning was at hand.

Mary Agatha came first to help Ruth lift Lucie out of bed for her morning needs. The woman sensed a cloud in the room and eyed Ruth curiously. "You sleep last night?" she asked. "You got circles 'round yer eyes like ya been cryin' or maybe been too close to the smokin' fire. Somethin' wrong, Sister Ruth?"

There's plenty wrong, thought Ruth, but she held her tongue. Mary Agatha was better off suspecting nothing.

Ruth suddenly heard Ez Brackett's voice and opened the door wide enough to see him stagger toward the fire pit, tipping his chin to Clara Tophorn and reaching for his cup. He was half clothed and ragged looking—a repulsive, brutish man—and Ruth had no regrets about what she'd done. He sat down heavily on the nearest log, and his eyes drifted toward the pathway and the cabin. Frightened, Ruth quickly closed the door but opened it again slightly when Brackett turned away.

Ruth heard Clara ask about her husband, Cal, as she poured his brother's coffee. "He was with ya out below," complained Clara. "How is it that ya don't know where he went?" Brackett mumbled something in return that didn't satisfy her. She ranted on while the big man sipped complacently at his cup, and Ruth's heart pounded as she watched and listened. She felt Mary Agatha beside her at the door and smiled, wishing she could tell her about the plan. *Would you like to watch your catnip work its will? Would you like to see what your fennel and butterfly weed can do to a man's stomach?* But Ruth said nothing, keeping her eyes glued on Ez Brackett as he nursed his coffee.

"What you lookin' at?" asked Mary Agatha, peering over Ruth. "Why, it's only Ez sippin' on his mornin' cup. You got nuthin' to worry about from him." She glanced suspiciously at Ruth and then nudged her aside. "Let me go get Lucie's mush 'fore them kids get up and eat it all."

Ruth let her out and watched her as she made her way down the path toward Clara and the fire. Brackett ignored her, ponderously watching the steam rise from his mug, but Clara dutifully spooned two globs of mush into Mary Agatha's kettle. "It's plenty hot," Clara warned, "an' them women might burn their tongues if they ain't careful. I got no cream to cool it. Cal's disappeared, an' the cow ain't been milked."

Suddenly, Brackett noticed Mary Agatha, and his eyes drifted once more in the direction of the cabin. He rose slowly to his feet. At the door of the hut, Ruth's heart leapt to her throat. No! She'd bar the entrance! She'd fight him with anything she had!

But Ez Brackett was on his way to Lucie's door, and there was nothing she could do. Then, before the man took another step, he paused and swayed slightly. Suddenly, he lost his balance as if some nausea had seized him. He looked blankly at the cup, which was still in his hand, and turned, bewildered and then angry, throwing it to the ground. "What the devil's in that coffee?" he thundered and lurched suddenly toward the trees and his own cave. Unable to walk a straight line, groaning as he stumbled, he pitched forward, barely able to crawl, aware of nothing, caring for nothing except finding a private place to double over and regurgitate.

Mary Agatha and Clara Tophorn both stood speechless as they watched Brackett finally rise and stagger away. "I hope Luke Royal ain't been messin' with that cup again," said Clara. "Heaven knows it warn't my coffee."

Gathering up the cup along with the mush, Mary Agatha slowly approached Ruth and the cabin. "Ya put somethin' in Ez's coffee, now didn't ya?" she chortled the moment she met Ruth's eyes. "Was it flax or common chickweed that ya used?"

"It was the catnip and fennel," admitted Ruth a little sheepishly. "I had to keep him away from Lucie for another few hours. Surely, you understand."

"Well, one or the other will prob'ly do it. The fennel will give 'im a gut ache, and the catnip'll let 'im sleep it off."

Ruth was relieved that Mary Agatha seemed to be applauding what she'd done until the woman added balefully, "He'll be ornery enough to kill when he wakes up."

Ruth stood her ground, suddenly defiant. "We won't be here when he wakes up. The Brethren are coming this morning. Cal Brackett's leading them straight here. Your people's crimes are over, Mary Agatha. Lucie's going home."

Mary Agatha paused to consider this. "What happens, happens," she shrugged. "I've done my best for both of you, I reckon." Then she began dishing up Lucie's mush in a tin bowl, carefully tasting it to check its temperature. "This is still plenty hot, and Clara's got no milk this mornin'." She handed Lucie the bowl with a pad to place it on. "Just let it cool a minute so as not to burn yer tongue."

Lucie crawled to the edge of the bed, putting one leg over the side and letting the other lay stiff across the blankets. "Thank you, Mary Agatha," she said and smiled at the woman. The success of the fennel tea in Ez Brackett's cup had delighted Lucie, and she focused her pleasure on Mary Agatha's mush.

The gesture gave the woman pause. She looked at Lucie and leaned over to pat her hand. "Remember now, let it cool a little." Then she turned to face Ruth, her deep-set eyes a mystery. "Ya took a big chance with them fennel leaves, Sister Ruth," she said. "Who knows how much they tickled Ez or just how long he'll sleep? There never is a promise that such things even work, dependin' on what they's mixed with. Ya took a chance all right, and nuthin's over yet. Who knows when yer folks'll come? Ya might a just stirred up a hornet's nest. Ya might get stung right good with nuthin' to show for it."

"No," said Ruth. "We'll be all right now. God's been with us all along."

The woman nodded. "He's always with ya, Sister Ruth, cuz yer His angel. I've never met no one like ya. The things ya done for that girl who ain't even yer own. The things ya read me in those books. The chances you've taken. Yer not of this world."

Ruth was embarrassed again and stepped outside with Mary Agatha. Taking in the morning air and her companion's smile, Ruth spoke deliberately. "There are many women far more saintly than I am, Mary. I want you to remember that. You've singled me out because you're not acquainted with the others."

"Them others don't know you," said Mary Agatha, and she turned away, moving rigidly down the path and skirting the center fires, where the Grovers, Gertie Royal, Clara Tophorn, and the children were having breakfast, unconcerned about the strange woman and her purposes.

Ruth sat down in the tiny room, where Lucie still held her steaming mush untouched. They shared a smile. "Let Mary think of you as an angel," said Lucie softly. "I know I do."

Filled with relief and joy, Ruth placed her hands on Lucie's shoulders and rocked her gently. "Oh, Lucie, my girl, I think we've made it through."

Seconds later, Ruth was at the table, ladling a bit of current juice for Lucie. If there was no milk for her mush, at least it could be sweetened, especially today. "The first thing we'll do is get you to a doctor," she mused, "probably in St. George, and then a specialist in Salt Lake as soon as we can get there."

Lucie was jubilant. "Do you suppose Albert knows what's happened? Do you think he'll meet the train?"

"Of course he will, and my Jesse too and at least some of my children. I want my Lucy Beryl to meet you. She has your name, and that's something to live up to. I won't mind telling her so, and when she sees you, she won't mind that I did."

They chatted like this—free and easy, two Mormon women who had shared so much. And Ruth stood with the ladle in her hand and thanked God for the moment.

Suddenly, from outside, a thudding sound burst through the reverie. The cabin door opened with a violent shudder, and there stood Ezra Brackett, filling the frame with his considerable bulk and peering bleary-eyed at Lucie as she slid back against the wall, still clutching her bowl of mush. Ruth dropped the ladle. It glanced noisily off the iron pot and bounced to the floor. For a split second, she was rigid, shocked into a stupor by Brackett's abrupt appearance. He was wretched looking and pale, but the tea's potency had been short-lived. Now, he was like a wounded animal, made more vicious by the pain. He scowled at Ruth and raged, "I told ya last night to clear out! What're ya still doin' here?"

Ruth couldn't breathe. When she moved at last, Brackett was already at the bedside, hovering over Lucie like a black shadow. "I've been up all night," he bellowed, "a stirrin' in my mind. Now I got a gut ache that won't quit, an' my tongue's on fire. It's you that's done this to me," he raged at the girl. "I don't figure to pace over it no longer. I got ya here to be a wife, and that's what yer gonna be!" Suddenly bending close to Lucie, Brackett's matted beard brushed her cheek as he pleaded, "Come on, now, give me a little kiss to soothe my pain and seal the bargain." As his dry lips sought her mouth, Lucie squealed and jerked away. Ruth jumped forward to grab the iron ladle, anything for a weapon, and she heard Lucie's tin bowl clatter to the floor. Brackett stumbled backward with a yelp, nearly losing his balance, and then stood stupefied staring at his hands and the front of his unbuttoned shirt. Thick mush covered his face from eyebrows to beard. It oozed through the hair on his bare chest. It was still hot enough to sting, and Brackett swiped at the worst of it as if he were slapping mosquitoes. "You little witch!" he garbled and then began to cough and sputter over the cereal in his mouth and nose. Lucie, backed flat against the wall, was trembling, but she held her head up, proud of what she'd done, and never took her eyes from Brackett's.

With the end of his shirt tail, the man made an effort to clean himself, but chunks of gooey mush were dribbling through his beard, leaving it matted and sticky. Roaring in frustration, he cleared the table with one long wave of his arm, sending jars and candles and dishes scattering. Then, eyes aflame, he turned to Ruth. "I'm gonna go wash up," he growled. "When I come back, I want all this stuff cleared out. All of it! The dishes and the sewin' and the seeds. I want it all cleared outta here. And I want you gone too! You, with yer fancy woman's talk and yer righteous ways. You clear on outta here! I'm takin' this girl to wife, an' there's nuthin' ya can do about it. Ya think yer high and mighty, that this girl's too good for me. You Mormons think yer better than us poor mountain folks. Well, I'm takin' what I want, and there ain't nuthin ya kin do about it!" He backed out with one last look at Lucie, and then he snarled again at Ruth, "Ten minutes, and you'd better be gone!" He left the door swinging on its rusty hinges as he barged through it, stomping away while he wiped his sticky chin.

Ruth sank down next to Lucie and took her in her arms. Lucie's eyes were wide and frightened, and she clung to her protector sobbing, "Go along, Sister Fox. I don't want you hurt on my account. I'll be all right."

Ruth was immediately on her feet. "Don't wither yet, Lucie," she said. "I'll just be gone a minute." She fled from the cabin to the main camp circle, where Clara and Gertie were still stirring the breakfast cooking fires and chattering about the "dirty" coffee cup. Ruth flew between the women and pleaded desperately, "I need a weapon! A carving knife! A pocket knife! Some kind of a blade. You must have something here!"

"We got a knife to cut up meat, but I ain't givin' it to you," said Clara while Gertie looked on blankly.

"Ez Brackett's comin' for Lucie!" cried Ruth, grabbing Clara's sleeve. "Surely, as a woman, you'll help me protect her!"

"Now, why would I butt in where I ain't wanted?" laughed Clara. "Ez got a right to have a wife. You think yer girl's too good fer 'im?"

"What ya need is a gun," put in Gertie smugly. "Ya shoulda kept the one ya had. We seen ya draggin' it behind the day ya come. A Henry rifle, as I recollect."

Ruth looked into Gertie's pinched face and saw mockery in her eyes. "Where is that gun?" she cried. "You've got to tell me."

"I'll tell ya where it is," said Clara, "for all the good it'll do ya. That half-wit Mary Agatha has it. She's had it since ya first come. Rootin' and putterin' around like a pack rat, the way she does. I seen her find that rifle in the lean-to when you was passed out. She's got it hidden away somewhere with ever'thin' else she's scavenged. You go talk crazy Agatha out of it if ya can."

Ruth whirled away and dashed back through the trees toward the cabin, searching frantically for Mary Agatha. Ruth could hardly believe that Mary had the rifle. Weren't they friends? Hadn't they bonded, almost like sisters? Wasn't the woman even a little bit of an ally in protecting Lucie? In a frenzy, Ruth looked in every direction. From where she stood, she scanned the pinion trees, the boulder caves, the crude trough of water near the spring, the pathway to the upward trail. Then, like a specter, Mary Agatha appeared before her, standing stiff and tall. Ruth grabbed her bony shoulders. "Mary, do you have the Henry rifle? I've got to have that rifle! Please, please tell me where it's hidden! Brackett's coming for Lucie, and I've got to have a gun!"

"You tol' me that rifle warn't loaded," said Mary Agatha sharply. "Ain't that what ya said?"

Ruth began pounding on the woman's arms with her tiny, useless fists. "I've got to have that gun!" she cried. "I can use it for a bluff even if it isn't loaded. I can threaten with it. I can bar the door. Please, Mary Agatha. I've got to keep that man away from Lucie if it's the last thing I ever do!"

Mary Agatha looked down at Ruth with a strange sympathy in her eyes. "I've got the rifle," she finally said softly, "but I cain't give it to ya. Yer a holy woman, an' I ain't lettin' ya shoot Ez Brackett. Besides, he's my kin, ya know. My brother's boy. You tend to strangers, Ruth. We take care of our own." With that, Mary Agatha pushed Ruth's hands away and turned abruptly to walk back up the path, leaving Ruth numb and speechless. There was nothing she could do.

At that same instant, Ez Brackett came stomping through the trees, heading straight toward Ruth and the cabin door. In only seconds he was next to her, bent on pushing her aside. Stubbornly, she faced him, ready to plead for reason, plead for time, but he snorted and threw her back without ever breaking stride. "I tol' ya to clear out!" he growled as he lumbered past her. Clamoring onto the back of his broad shoulders, screaming for him to stop, Ruth wound her arm around his neck, and when he shook her off and left her rolling on the ground, she grabbed his boot and ankle and held on while he dragged her through the dirt, finally kicking himself free. Ruth rose to her knees, still screaming, and then she helplessly watched Ez Brackett barge through Lucie's door.

In a flood of apocalyptic light, Ruth saw Lucy Beryl, dancing on a cloud, her cheeks aglow, her ribboned braids leaping off her back, her dress of ivory lace elegant in the sun. Oh, the beauty of youth, of innocence, of hope. How many journeys had Ruth made in the name of virtue? All for nothing? Lucie Cole *was* her Lucy Beryl. The girl was every Lucie, every Susan, every Meg. And, try as she might, in the end, Ruth couldn't save them by herself.

The rifle shot cracked the air like the snapping of a whip—lethal, precise, and coming out of nowhere. Jolted to her senses, Ruth looked on in horror as Ez Brackett was knocked backward in his tracks and fell without another sound in front of the little hut, a single bullet between his eyes. Ruth's hands flew to her mouth as she gasped. There were no words to utter.

She stumbled forward to where the man lay, a motionless giant in the sand, pierced by one small stone. Mary Agatha came from the door of the hut, dragging the Henry rifle behind her, and looked at the body with casual interest. "Ya wuz right about the bullet left in the barrel," she said indifferently and bent to help Ruth to her feet.

Ruth grabbed the woman's arm and rose slowly. Her eyes, wide with disbelief, met Mary's empty glance. "You . . . you wouldn't let me do it," she whispered. "Five minutes ago, you wouldn't let me do it."

Mary Agatha looked again at Ez Brackett sprawled out before them. When she turned back to Ruth, her eyes were glowing. "Yer still a holy woman, Sister Ruth. Thar's no blood on yer hands. Ya ain't tainted by this man, an' neither is poor Lucie."

"What made you . . . ?" Ruth was still in shock.

"Remember how God spoke to Nephi in the book and tol' him to kill that fella Laban, his own kin, to save somethin' precious? Well, this time God spoke to me."

Ruth dropped Mary Agatha's hand and looked about. Clara and Gertie, the Grovers, Jacob Royal, and the children—everyone in the camp milled around them, awestricken, looking curiously from Mary Agatha to stiff Ez Brackett lying on the ground.

Ruth left them all gawking and murmuring among themselves. In the cabin, a shaken Lucie Cole sat sobbing on the bed, and Ruth fell beside her and embraced her, calming her tenderly with love and approbation. Their long ordeal was over, thanks to Tom Leavitt's Henry rifle and a Book of Mormon story that an old gray-haired woman didn't know how to read.

Chapter Fourteen
EPILOGUE

LATER THAT MORNING, SO THE story goes, Jennings Burton and his troop showed up on the mountain. Cal Brackett, still confused and deluded, led them through the slot canyon to the cluttered hideaway where his vagabond family waited. The spirit chasers offered no resistance as the sheriffs from two counties, together with their deputies and the Church detectives, rounded up the "family" and sifted through the stolen goods that could be identified. The doctor, who'd left his buggy at the base of the incline, hiked to the site with his bag and hurried first to Lucie Cole. Recognizing immediately that her leg required more specialized attention, he had her carried out as soon as the fastest team was ready.

"Take her to Cedar City first," he ordered. "There's a doctor there named Bloom. Get him on the case, and send word to Salt Lake for a surgeon to be ready—and be quick about it."

"My gosh," said Sheriff Booker, "you ladies cheated the devil here. Tom Leavitt would be proud."

Ruth moved with Lucie's stretcher to the slot and kissed her cheek as the men prepared to lift her into the waiting wagon below. The girl clung to the woman's wrist until the last. "Oh, Sister Ruth," she wept. "Please . . . you won't leave me for long?"

"I'll be right behind you on the road," Ruth assured her. "You go ahead with the Brethren now. They'll get you to a doctor who'll take care of you."

"You'll see me in Salt Lake?" Lucie pleaded one last time, and Ruth nodded emphatically as their hands parted and the stretcher moved away.

Dr. Morgan, who remained behind, offered medical treatment to everyone, from sunburned, lice-infested children to Levi Grover, who had a bleeding ulcer. Though Dr. Morgan did have more advanced drugs to offer, he was impressed with Mary Agatha's work and her array of natural medicines. "She's actually saved lives," he told Ruth. "These folks were lucky she was here."

"So was I," Ruth murmured.

Ruth had recognized her old friend Jennings Burton the minute the first members of the posse appeared, and she greeted him with a grateful embrace. "I knew the Church would send the best it had," she said. "And how is Fenton Meade? I was sure the Lord would help him make it to Modena."

"He made it," said Burton, "and it looks like you did too." The General Authority kindly wiped her dusty, tearstained cheek with his thumb. "Good golly, Ruth! What's Jesse gonna say? He won't ever let you travel for the Church again!"

"Jesse knows where I'm needed," answered Ruth. "He'll get over this."

She and Burton and some of the other men walked quietly and curiously around Ez Brackett's body, and Ruth explained how she'd had to follow him into the desert, afraid of losing sight of Lucie or their footprints if she stayed behind. She told them about Mary Agatha and about the Henry rifle and the bullet in the pipe. She confessed that, while Mary Agatha was the one who killed Ez Brackett, she would have pulled the trigger herself if she'd had the chance. "The woman thinks I'm somehow holy because I've shed no blood," she told Jennings Burton later, "but heaven knows I tried."

Some of the men stayed behind to sort through what was in the camp and decide how best to handle the spirit chasers who had committed no crime—the women and the children. In the following days, they were taken off the mountain to be fed and sheltered in Modena until all charges were settled. Some of them would eventually find work in St. George and Cedar City, where their children were sent to school. Others drifted back to the wilderness, which was their right if they wanted to weather the hardship, so long as they didn't steal or let their children go hungry. Some believe that Gertie and Jacob Royal eventually lived outside Kanab, where Jacob led a spiritual congregation. Cal Brackett never quite recovered from his head injuries and died before the age of forty in Pima, Arizona, where Clara and her children settled. The deputies had buried his brother Ezra by the side of his first wife, Elsie, in the next draw over, where the ground was soft. There was little ceremony and no mourners. The freighter Tom Leavitt, on the other hand, was laid to rest under the trees in the St. George Cemetery, where a thousand people came to pay their last respects.

On the train home to Salt Lake City, Ruth asked Jennings Burton not to publicize her and Lucie's ordeal. "Just let it fade away," she said. "It's something Lucie would just as soon forget, I'm sure. Once her leg heals, her life can begin again with only her Albert to think about."

"What about you, Ruth?" asked Burton. "Is this something you can just let go?"

"No, but it's a private matter. I think I'd rather keep the memories to myself, at least for the next hundred years!"

Of course, Ruth never forgot Mary Agatha, who spent her latter days in Modena, where she became well-known for her natural medicines. Many a sagebrush family sought her out when they had nowhere else to turn, and it was said that hundreds owed their lives to her rustic prairie wisdom. Before Ruth left the mountain the day she was rescued, she and Mary walked alone together one last time through the harsh rock pilings and the cedar trees. "Yer a holy woman," Mary Agatha insisted. "I never knew no one like ya, and I swear one day I'm gonna figure what makes a person God's own angel right here on this earth. Maybe it's in that book of yers, that Book of Mormon. Someday I'll learn to read it better an' find out."

"You do that, Mary!" Ruth laughed heartily but with pent-up tears in her eyes. "You read every word!"

"I'm sorry I lied to you about the gun," said the woman sheepishly. "I couldn't let you have it, Sister Ruth. I'd gotten feelings for you and Lucie, 'specially towards the end, and guns is dangerous, ya know. When it come right down to it, I knew I had to take things into my own hands to save you. You mighta hurt yerself."

Ruth looked at her strange friend, and her voice cracked as she spoke. "You *did* save us, Mary." Silently, she kissed the woman's cheek. "I want you to remember that. Like Nephi and David, you did what you had to do. Don't let the killing canker your soul."

"Yer soul wuz the one that needed to be pure," Mary Agatha answered plaintively, "for all the good it's yet to do."

***

Ruth May Fox never spoke publically about these events nor did anyone for many years. Ruth and her husband, Jesse, and their daughter Lucy Beryl attended many wedding celebrations in Salt Lake City the summer and fall of 1903. Surely those included the marriage of Mr. and Mrs. Albert Covington, where Ruth's embrace of the bride held special meaning and the groom looked as jaunty and handsome as his picture in the silver case.

The nuptials had to be postponed until September while the bride recovered from an injury, but the wedding was the highlight of the season when it finally came about. As Lucie's mother had planned, music floated through a house bedecked with fall flowers. Aunt Caroline and half a dozen girls from Dixie were among the wedding guests. Ruth never mentioned the celebration in her journal, though, nor the days she and Lucie spent as captives in the little cabin. She traveled the earth for the next fifty years—from Europe to Hawaii and back again—and never spoke of it.

Perhaps the legend of her time among the spirit chasers of the Southern Utah desert is just a myth. Or maybe it's a metaphor for her devotion to the young women of the Church who needed her guidance and protection against the stalkers of this world and the ever-present dangers that they symbolize: temptation, immorality, selfishness, all the sins that stalk good people at one time or another. The Grand Lady certainly warned her girls against these things. Was there a real Ezra Brackett to threaten a real Lucie Cole? Does it matter? What we do know for sure is that Sister Ruth May Fox "carried on" and lived to fly in airplanes on her Church assignments, as Jennings Burton had predicted.

Since the story of Ruth's ordeal on the desert was never written down—until now—perhaps it didn't really happen. But Ruth *was* in

Southern Utah in 1903, traveling for the Church in a wagon behind a team of horses. Her diary describes the end of the trip this way:

Wed. 16 Drove about 15 miles taking dinner with Bro. and Sister Holt. In the afternoon traveled to Modena 25 miles, making in all by team about 300 miles. By rail when we reach home, over 500. Attended 35 meetings and spoke in 22.

Thur. 17 Reached home this morning finding everything all right.

A long journey for Sister Fox, hundreds of dusty miles, and everything all right at home. Maybe nothing happened on the road to Modena that year except a routine stop for dinner with the Holts. Then again, who knows?

About the Author

LYNNE LARSON IS A MUCH-PUBLISHED author of stories and articles related to religion, history, and literature. The pioneer Church and especially its women is a theme of special interest. A retired teacher, she devotes her time to promoting education in the humanities, as well as a love of Western history, at every opportunity. She is a graduate of Brigham Young University and holds a master's degree in English from Idaho State University in Pocatello. She and her husband, Kent, are the parents of three grown children.